My Story

D0167025

THE GREAT PLAGUE

Pamela Oldfield

Scholastic Canada Ltd.
Toronto New York London Auckland Sydney
Mexico City New Delhi Hong Kong Buenos Aires

CH 08113

While the events described and some of the characters in this book may be based on actual historical events and real people, Alice Paynton is a fictional character, created by the author, and her diary is a work of fiction.

Library and Archives Canada Cataloguing in Publication
Oldfield, Pamela
The great plague : a London girl's diary / Pamela Oldfield.
(My story)
ISBN 978-0-545-98547-5
1. Great Plague, London, England, 1664-1666--Juvenile fiction.
I. Title. II. Series: My story (Toronto, Ont.)
PZ7.O528Gr 2009   j823'.914   C2008-906822-X

Off Leather Lane, London
1665

May 9th, 1665

Tuesday. Today I start my new diary and have a new hiding place for it — behind a beam in the ceiling of my attic bedchamber. There was a small gap which I have made larger with my fingers. No one will find it. The old diary rests deep in my clothes chest at the bottom of the bed. I am fortunate that we live in such a pleasant house. Some families are crammed into one room. If I had to share a bedchamber I could have no secrets.

I start with the news that Papa promises to take us to the Dukes Theatre to see a play called *Mustapha*. That is, myself, Papa and Aunt Nell who is my mother's older sister. My mother, Letitia, died when I was born but I have her dark hair and the same grey eyes. When I was younger I wanted to call Aunt Nell "Mama." 'Twas merely a childish pretence but she would have none of it.

So . . . my first play. Thank you, Papa.

Tomorrow down to Woolwich by water and carrier to spend two days on Uncle John's farm. Aunt Nell has made a vast tray of gingerbread by way of a gift. I have bought an ivory ring for the newest child to cut his teeth on.

3

Maggie's neighbour in St Giles (Maggie is our live-in maidservant) has the spotted fever and they think she will die.

May 11th

Two days later and I am home in my beloved London. (I never take my diary to Uncle John's for fear of prying eyes. Too many children.) Returned from Woolwich with the tide and with a most pleasing waterman. I do believe the cheeky wretch found me to his fancy tho' such a man would never do for me. But he winked at me when Aunt Nell's gaze was busy elsewhere on the water and I feared a blush would betray me. Aunt Nell, however, noticed nothing.

But thank Heavens 'twas only a short visit. Uncle John's children are noisy, boisterous souls, bless them, and the new baby bawls for hours at a time. I gave him the ivory ring but he threw it on the floor. Aunt Mary says she will give it to him when he is older as his teeth are not coming through yet. I grumble yet they are kindly folk and all the family I have on Papa's side. Uncle John is very like Papa but fatter and with more hair. Cousin Annie's limp is less obvious than last time I saw her. She was born with uneven legs. Aunt Mary claimed at first that a local witch had put the evil eye on her but Aunt

4

Nell spoke to her with great patience to dispel the notion. Now the cobbler has made Annie a shoe with a thick heel and sole for the short leg. She is a sunny child and makes little of it and Aunt Mary is content.

Uncle John sent us home as usual loaded with food. I think he believes that town dwellers are always underfed. He gave us three rabbits fresh from the snares, a basket of eggs and two jars of honey from his bees. I kept well away for fear of being stung again. The honey pleased Aunt Nell for sugar is costly and she has such a sweet tooth.

I learned a most shameful secret from Cousin Kate who is now eighteen. She has no husband but she is with child. The child's father is from Newcastle — a seaman on a coalship. They will wed in haste when he next docks in London. She says he is short and scarred from the smallpox but has a sunny disposition. His name is Jem. I shall never have a child out of wedlock for fear of Papa's anger. Uncle John forbade Kate to speak of it to anyone so I dare not tell Aunt Nell. (But have told Maggie.)

Aunt Mary teased me again about my distrust of horses. To prove her wrong I rode the big bay but fell off on to some hay which made them all laugh. Even Aunt Nell laughed which disappointed me greatly. If I never ride a horse again 'twill be too soon.

I milked one of the cows but the wretched animal was determined to kick over the pail. Farm work is not at all to my liking. Thank Heavens Papa is not a farmer.

5

Uncle John's old servant Hannah died the day we arrived. She was 49 — a good age — and died in her own bed a half mile away. Aunt Mary told the bees. She went to the hive and whispered the news and fastened a ribbon of black crepe to the top of the hive. Intrigued, I asked little Beth why she did all this.

"If we do not tell the bees they will fly away or die of grief," she said.

Next day

It is good to be back in London. (The first thing I did was to buy a mutton pie from the pie man and share it with Poppet.) I missed the bustle of the town, the clatter of hooves on cobbles and the cries of the streetsellers. Aunt Nell thinks I am mad. She would move to a cottage in the country if it were possible. She finds the countryside peaceful. Dull, I say. Such a life would not please me. The city is full of life and colour which I have known and loved all my days.

I have a large bruise on my thigh from my fall yesterday. A little more hay would have saved me. 'Tis no laughing matter. I might well have fallen on my head and split my skull.

May 13th

An unlucky day for me. Aunt Nell found a splinter in her thumb and called upon me to take it out. It was stubborn and I was forced to probe deep. She knows how much I hate to do this. It turns my stomach to see her wince. I never could become a doctor or physician.

May 15th

Brushed Poppet who most ungratefully nipped my hand. But he looks very fine and silky. Aunt Nell said I should bath him but he hates it so. I said I would do it in a day or two.

"A stitch in time . . ." she said, as I knew she would.

May 16th

Papa was in a sombre mood this evening. He spoke with Aunt Nell in a whisper and told me to pay no attention. Aunt Nell called me "a little pitcher with big ears," but I am thirteen and no longer a child. If something bad is happening I should be told.

I went to the kitchen in a fit of sulks. Maggie is sixteen and she alone treats me as an equal. She told me they speak of the plague and that the news is bad. Plague is come into England from across the water. A year ago it was in Holland and it has been in Italy and elsewhere.

"And now 'tis here," she said. "In London. Thirty-two folk died in St Giles in the Fields in the past seven days."

"Of the plague?" I asked, shocked.

She shrugged. "Most pretend 'tis the spotted fever but the authorities have sent women in as 'searchers' to discover the truth."

I found it hard to sleep then, for fear of what might befall our great city.

May 17th

Aunt Nell has come by a new recipe for an ointment to soothe scalds and burns. Unfortunately Maggie was busy washing, with a buck tub full of bed linen. It fell to me to make up the ointment. I spent an hour boiling hog's fat to clarify it. Meanwhile I separated two yolks from the whites of two eggs and then beat this latter into the cooled hog's fat which was not easy. I complained at length that my wrist ached and was told sharply that I was "no longer a child." (Praise be someone has realized that at last.) Then, "Put it in your book of household remedies," says Aunt Nell. Which means I must copy it out in my best handwriting. A tiresome task and not to my liking. And shall I ever use the wretched book? I am thirteen and have no admirers. How shall I come by a home of my own if all men do is wink at me from the far end of a boat?

I was so bored that I offered to help Maggie hang out the sheets but she grumbled that I let the sheet drag on the ground and dirtied it again. Hardly a day to remember. Perhaps I should only write up a good day. But then it might be a very thin diary.

9

May 18th

Maggie is in a strange mood and I pressed her for a reason.

"If the plague is come I shall surely succumb," she told me mournfully, "for I am accursed."

"Accursed? But why? How?"

"I was born on January the 30th, in 1649 — the day they beheaded King Charles."

Poor soul. I do not envy her such a birthday.

May 20th

I fretted all day about the plague and could not concentrate on my crochet work. That horrid little collar. I swear I shall never wear it. I muddled the stitches until Aunt Nell quite lost patience with me. I wanted to talk of the plague but feared to put it into words. I cannot believe that calamity is just around the corner. I was born in London and have lived here all my life. We cannot have the plague here. Imagine what would become of us if the King were to take the sickness and die. Surely God will not allow it. I trust the rumours are simply that — rumours with no real substance to them.

May 21st

Lordsday. Mighty warm for May. After church Aunt Nell persuaded Papa to let us go upriver to walk and air ourselves. He should come too, she said, and bring his fishing rod. He declined, pleading work, and said we should go without him, taking Maggie.

"You want to be rid of the womenfolk," Aunt Nell teased and he did not deny this.

We packed a basket of food before he could change his mind, and set off. The river looked so serene 'twas hard to recall that two years before the water rose until it flooded Whitehall. And that in late autumn it is frequently hidden by a dense smoke-laden fog. Today it flowed smoothly, glittering with sunlight and was full of traffic in both directions. Wherries and skiffs as ever but plenty more craft, some smaller, some larger.

We were overtaken at one point by an elegant boat full of rich courtiers. We were fortunate to see them for next month the Court retires to Oxford to avoid the midsummer heat. Also on board was a small ensemble of viols and lutes playing popular airs. Music on the water. We were all enchanted by it. Papa would have enjoyed it.

"Your father would have sung his heart out," said Aunt Nell.

True, I thought. Papa fancies himself as a singer and is in truth a pleasing baritone. She told me once that he and my mother used to sing together in the evenings.

"Letty's favourite was 'Greensleeves,'" she said, smiling at the memory.

"'Greensleeves' is also mine," I told her, tho' I had not known it until that very moment.

I wish I could picture the two sisters together before I came along to put an end to their joy. I try to imagine Papa as an earnest suitor or as a young man flushed with the novelty of wedded bliss. But sadly I cannot.

Seeing so many wherries filled with passengers I feared the riverbanks would be overcrowded. Crowded they were but not so much that we could not find a place to step ashore. We moored at the special spot where Letty and Nell used to walk with *their* mother — and a brother now dead. I always wonder if my mother's spirit lingers there and might come close to me. Would I know it if she did? Would I feel anything?

We had taken cold chicken and a vegetable salad with one of Aunt Nell's home-made loaves. We drank Uncle John's cider and finished with a custard tart. We could scarce move afterwards. Aunt Nell dozed beneath a tree and Maggie and I wandered among the fields picking buttercups and making daisy chains. We stayed well clear of a herd of cows and also of some hogs rootling beneath a stand of oak trees. Two gentlemen rode by on horses and raised their caps to us. I liked the one with fair hair and a roving eye but Maggie preferred the older man who was swarthy looking and not at all to my taste.

"They are father and son," I teased. "I shall wed the younger man. That leaves you the father!"

Maggie pretended to be shocked. "My, my, Alice Paynton. You are growing up apace," and we both fell to giggling.

'Twas fortunate Aunt Nell could not hear us.

We came home around four o'clock, very satisfied with our excursion.

May 22nd

Monday. Nothing of note. Aunt Nell was in a bad mood this evening because of a ruined skirt. She went to visit a friend in Southwark this morning and returned at low tide to find the landing stairs thick with mud. The surly waterman refused to help her out of the boat and she slipped and almost fell into the water. Incensed, she refused to pay her fare and marched

13

from the waterside with his strident curses ringing in her ears. Maggie has washed the petticoat but we can only wait for the skirt to dry so it might be brushed clean of the worst of the mud.

Master Ruddiard came for my singing lesson. I cannot resist his kindly blue eyes and sang scales for him until I longed to scream with boredom. But he promises to bring a new song sheet for me next time he comes. We shall see if he remembers.

May 24th

It seems the searchers have discovered many trickeries. There are numerous cases of plague unreported and Papa says an outbreak is inevitable. Aunt Nell says we must put our trust in the Lord and he will provide. Papa shakes his head and sighs. Aunt Nell says that he lost his faith when my mother died giving birth to me. But I have no such awful memories and will not be cast down by gloomy predictions. On Sunday I shall pray long and hard in church and put my trust in God.

Next day

I write this while my head throbs. I sat with Maggie for nigh on an hour this evening as she struggled with her writing. She forms the letters slowly but at least she can write after a fashion. Papa says this is progress. She came to us three years ago with no skills at all — unless you count beating the carpets half to death. She has strong arms and broad shoulders which come in useful since we have no manservant. Aunt Nell has taught her to read a little and poor Maggie labours over the Bible half an hour at a time. I confess I tire of the writing lessons but Papa says 'tis to our credit to have an educated servant. Aunt Nell says it teaches me patience (which I do not care to learn). I also know that (God willing) I shall one day need to teach my own children to read and write.

May 26th

The tuner came today for the virginals. He said the warm weather does them no good and the smoke from winter fires discolours the keys. And he has increased his price. Papa was not best pleased when he returned from the office.

Maggie snapped at me this morning. She has a toothache and used so much oil of cloves that Aunt Nell sent her to the apothecary to fetch more. Then she spent twenty minutes turning the spit for the chicken (a good thing 'twas not a larger one) and complained about the heat from the fire. She suggested that we make Poppet run round in a wheel to turn the spit. I was so put out I did not speak to her until the evening when she apologized.

May 27th

Maggie is in a bad mood again today and has put me quite out of humour. This afternoon I picked up the leather

16

bucket in the yard and found a dead rat in it. I screamed and dropped the bucket and Maggie called me a ninny. I doubt that she would have been one wit braver than I, faced with such a horrid sight. She said it had most likely died of the plague and I was half minded to tell Aunt Nell but I thought better of it for we are not to speak of the plague for fear it brings bad luck.

If Maggie leaves us the new servant might be worse. At least we are friends most of the time.

May 28th

Lordsday. Went to church — to our own pew in St Andrew's — and on the way watched some jugglers in the street which made us late. One of them had a humorous way with words and was entertaining the crowd. Even Aunt Nell laughed at his jokes. I should like to marry a man who makes me laugh and keeps me from melancholy. A man who shall never snap at me or call me careless (as Aunt Nell does) or complain about my singing (like Papa) or be unkind about my dog (like Maggie).

May 29th

A great scandal has broken in court of which Papa heard the details from Master Pepys himself. On Friday last, the Lord Rochester attempted to elope with a certain Mrs Mallet who is both beautiful and rich. She was snatched from her carriage, by prior arrangement, and bundled into another. The Lord Rochester himself was fast in pursuit of her but was seized and now languishes in The Tower for his sins. 'Tis said the King is most displeased.

"And what news of Mrs Mallet?" I asked.

"None of the lady," said Papa. "She has been spirited away."

" 'Tis none of our business," said Aunt Nell. "You ask too many questions."

Papa merely shrugged.

" 'Twill all end in tears!" said Aunt Nell, tut-tutting.

My aunt, bless her, has no romance in her soul. For my part, I think it the most romantic thing I have ever heard. A fair lady kidnapped and stolen away and a passionate man imprisoned for love of her. Papa shook his head in disapproval (he has that look to perfection) but I shall pray

18

for the lovers to be reunited. I confess I felt like cheering at the news. These excitements are the very stuff of London life. How can the country compare with such a town? For countryfolk no doubt a runaway ox or a thatch on fire is the best excitement they can hope for.

May 30th

Tuesday. No more news of the runaway lady but the Lord Rochester is still in The Tower. And still has his head, as Maggie remarked. 'Tis hardly a treasonable offence but 'twould be sad to see his head on a stake above London Bridge with those of criminals.

And now for a most secret thing. Papa must never know. Today Maggie has told me of a famous fortune-teller who has hung out his sign near Leadenhall market. He claims he is a distant cousin of Mother Shipton, the witch from the north. While not being evil in any way he is able to see into the future. I am determined to visit him to know for certain that, should the plague overtake us, we shall all survive.

June 2nd

More excitement but of a different nature. Papa tells us about the English fleet which should shortly be engaging the Dutch ships which greatly outnumber ours. I suggested the numbers may be exaggerated but Papa is adamant. If Master Pepys says 'tis so then 'tis so, for Papa hangs on his every word. Papa is so proud that he works for the Navy Board.

To please him I went to St Paul's with Aunt Nell this morning to pray on our knees for our brave sailors and to ask God to bring England a great victory.

"I fear the Dutch may be praying also," I whispered to Aunt Nell. "What is God to do?"

She nudged me hard with her elbow and hissed that I was blasphemous.

A letter has come from Uncle John, urging that Aunt Nell and I should join them in Woolwich if the plague takes hold in the city. Papa says it would be wise but Aunt Nell is against the notion. I am also. Weeks or even months with that noisy family. My nerves would be in tatters. I can enjoy them for a few days but longer would be a torment. And if we should go, who will care for Papa? Maggie can do little in the kitchen without supervision and how would Papa endure a daily breakfast of hardboiled eggs and burnt toast?

I wish folk would not harp on so about the plague. I know that Holland was stricken two years since and that thousands died but 'tis years since London suffered. I think we must visit that man in Leadenhall market who can tell the future. That would put my fears at rest.

June 3rd

My naughty little Poppet escaped again today and I was in a turmoil searching the streets until I found him two doors away from home. He had chased Mistress Capperly's ginger cat into the house and she was most displeased. She insisted that I take more care of my pet.

"If the plague increases, dogs at large in the streets will be seized and killed," she said.

I hope she is wrong.

Today I learned another great secret by way of Aunt Nell. Papa is to buy me a string of pearls for my fourteenth birthday. It will look well with the ring my grandmother left me — seed pearls in a gold band which suits my slim hand to perfection, tho' I say it myself. Only two more months to go.

A string of pearls. I can hardly believe my good fortune. If I close my eyes I can almost feel them resting against my throat. I do believe I am the happiest young woman in the world.

June 4th

Lordsday. In church with Papa to give thanks for the victory at sea. Yesterday we heard the guns all day and England put the Dutch to flight. But there were heavy losses. Came home early before the sermon as Papa had a bad attack of colic. He went to bed and Aunt Nell dosed him with mint tea to ease his stomach. Around six Papa's colleague Master Waybold called on us with news of yesterday's battle. It seems the Earl of Falmouth was killed outright with one shot which killed two others also. And some admirals are also lost. We took many of their best ships and lost no more than 700 men while killing nigh on 10,000 of theirs. Ten thousand? I wondered if this could possibly be true but Master Waybold insisted it 'twas so. Papa says 'twas the greatest sea battle of all time.

"But 10,000?" I repeated. "The sea must be full of bodies!"

Papa gave me an angry look and I waited for Aunt Nell to mutter "Doubting Thomas" but she refrained. I said I would pray for *all* their souls and retired to the kitchen to tell Maggie.

22

June 5th

Most wonderful excitement. Maggie has a sweetheart now and to hear her you would imagine him a god at the very least.

"Write that in your diary," she told me with a wicked smile. "Write that he takes the most glorious liberties."

I asked what these liberties were but she laughed, tossed her head and patted that glorious golden hair.

How I wish I were more like her — in looks, that is, not situation. It seems this young god goes by the name of Jon Ruddle and he is a waterman on the Thames like his father and grandfather before him. Maggie says he has the bluest eyes and hair like silk. She is clearly besotted with him. I must admit I was envious to hear that he has kissed her. I wish Master Ruddiard would try to kiss me (tho' I would not allow it). He did once put his hand on my midriff when teaching me how to breathe but Aunt Nell was present and gave a little cough. He snatched his hand away and blushed to the roots of his hair. He tells me that I sing like an angel. If only Papa thought so. He complains that my voice shows no improvement and that he is throwing his money away on my lessons. Last week he bid me sing for him. I gave him "As At Noon Dulcina Rested" (which

Aunt Nell declared was prettily done) and then "Come Live With Me And Be My Love". I imagined myself to be lovesick Maggie and sang it most heartfelt but Papa was not impressed. I cannot please him whatever I do. 'Tis truly vexing.

June 6th

In a dark mood all day. Papa has cancelled our visit to the theatre for fear of the plague in crowded places. 'Tis said that the gaming houses will soon be closed and the music houses also. I sat in my room all day and would speak to no one. Aunt Nell says I could win a prize for my sulks. No one understands me. No one cares. Why am I cursed with such a family?

Next day

Maggie's brother Will called in today while Aunt Nell was at the shops. (She cannot bear him in the house, calling him a young thief, which is true.) We let him into the kitchen and gave him a slice of caraway cake. He could do with a bath and some shoes but Maggie says he is used to going barefoot. He has the most cheerful disposition and seems to find the world a place of endless amusement. For an eight year old he is remarkably quick. Or maybe I should say quick-fingered for he pocketed one of our silver spoons and Maggie had to run after him down the street, hollering at him to return it. I hastened after them. (Aunt Nell would have a fit to see me run in the street.) Maggie only caught him because he cannoned into an elderly gentleman who grabbed him by the collar of his shirt and gave him a good shaking. Maggie gave him a clout but he laughed and put out his tongue. I do wish I had a brother or sister but when my mother died, Papa swore he would never wed again. Aunt Nell claims that living without a wife has made him short-tempered. Amen to that, I say, for something surely has. If I have a husband and he dies I shall most certainly wed again.

June 8th

Have finished the collar and will never crochet another. I have hid it in my chest and hope never to set eyes on it again. Such fiddly work is not at all to my taste tho' Aunt Nell claims it is good for my temper.

" 'Twill do you good, Alice, to slow down and concentrate," she tells me again and again.

" 'Twill drive me to distraction," I reply and she pretends to be shocked and tries not to smile. I wonder if Mama would have been like her had she lived. She is the kindest creature but a mite too strict. Mama was two years younger and her hair was darker. Aunt Nell says that I am truly made in her image.

June 9th

A day to remember. I met Maggie's sweetheart, Jon. We were shopping together and he was on his way to the river. He does have very blue eyes but his hair was tousled and lacked a comb. He put his arm round Maggie's waist and kissed her tho' she pretended to push him away. He is full of talk of the plague and frightened us with a dreadful story.

"I have this fare a day back," he told us, "who staggers as he comes down the steps. Drunk, I think to meself. He asks to be taken to Southwark but I've gotten a good look at him by this time. I'm a bit uneasy, like. I wants to refuse but then he offers me twice the usual fare. When I still hesitate he doubles that, so I think, 'Take a chance, my lad.' "

Maggie said, " 'Twas mighty rash, Jon."

26

"But I did," he told her. "By the time he's sat in the boat he's shivering and white as death. Suddenly he empties his belly all over the boat. Ugh! I'm tempted to throw him overboard but fear to overturn the boat. By the time we fetch up on the far side he can scarcely climb out. I won't help him for fear of touching him and he slips and falls in and is carried away."

There was a long silence.

He said, "I saw no tokens, Maggie. I swear it. But I made a pretty penny." He patted his pocket.

"Tokens?" Maggie said.

"Aye. Those dark spots beneath the skin. Tokens is a sure sign of plague."

"Is he drowned then?" I asked. "This man?"

"Your guess is as good as mine."

Maggie had gone very pale. She said, "You must steep the coins in vinegar. That way you'll be safe from contagion."

"I did that, don't you fret, my lamb. And swilled out the boat." He grinned. "I'll be rich by the time this is all over. How d'you fancy being wed to a rich man, eh?"

And he gave her another kiss. I must confess, I was glad he wasn't kissing me. As we made our way homeward we agreed not to repeat what we had heard for fear Papa will send us down to Woolwich.

June 10th

I dare not tell Papa but Maggie and I visited the fortune-teller. We found the place easily enough by the line of people who waited outside to see him. Once inside we found ourselves in a strange room. 'Twas draped with dark fabrics and there were mystic signs on the wall. There was no window that we could see and the smell was foul. We were both a little frightened but would not admit it. The man himself was small and wizened and his hair was grey and straggled over his collar. His eyes were small, dark and piercing and his clothes were magical — a long black robe decorated with silver moons. And he smelled mightily of garlic. He took my money and asked my date of birth, then consulted a large chart which was pinned out flat on a table. The chart was covered with a confusion of coloured shapes — I could only identify a few. A star, a horse with a man's head, a black sun, a green triangle and two crossed arrows. Thick black lines linked the various shapes in a somewhat random fashion. The fortune-teller slid a gnarled forefinger across the parchment, pausing at each symbol. He muttered to himself, wrinkling his face into a frown.

Unable to bear the silence I asked, "Are the signs good? Will we survive?"

In a quavering voice, he informed me that the signs were mainly good but still uncertain and I should return in a week's time for a more accurate reading, "When the stars are in a more propitious conjunction."

Suppressing niggling doubts I tried to take this as most positive but Maggie was sceptical.

"And then you will ask her to return yet again, no doubt!" she told him. "A fig for your prediction!"

Then she dragged me outside and told the waiting people to save their hard-earned money. All but one ignored her. The last, an elderly woman, shook her head sadly and wandered away.

"They are buying hope," I told Maggie, more than a little mortified.

"They are being cheated!" she returned. "He is nothing but a stinking charlatan."

I fear she was right but I blamed her for putting the idea into my head and said so. We walked home in silence, at odds with each other.

I hate Saturdays. Papa is at home and looking for faults in all of us. Today was worse than usual. He claimed my fingernails were not clean enough, told Maggie that she eats too much and accused Aunt Nell of squandering his money.

June 11th

Sunday. St Andrew's held special prayers for those suffering with the plague, which made me most fearful. While we were at church Uncle John called at the house with a brace of partridges, a basket of fresh vegetables and a barrel of his best cider. But he was in haste to get back to Woolwich and would not wait for our return. Maggie says he was "all a twitter" in fear of the contagion. It seems there are fresh cases in the liberties to the west of the city wall and fine weather will bring more. God help them all. It seems that the contagion likes the heat so we must hope for a cool summer.

June 13th

Mistress Capperly called by to tell us of a certain way to ward off the plague. A walnut shell filled with mercury is worn on a leather lace around the neck. She was wearing one herself, which she had bought from a stall on the steps of St

Paul's. Aunt Nell was ready to hasten there at once but when we told Papa he was against the notion, saying that it was a sop for the gullible. He has been told on the best authority (a colleague in the Navy Board, no less) that a void in the stomach allows the pestilential humours to enter and we should eat frequently of eggs and strong pickles.

June 14th

Ten o'clock has just struck. I am quite worn out and write this diary in bed. Papa is below entertaining Master Waybold and his new wife. Maggie and I shopped all morning and all afternoon helped Aunt Nell to prepare the supper. The weather being hot the kitchen was like an oven with the fire lit. We made a salad with young spinach leaves and lettuce hearts, white endive and chervil. It looked well spread on the plate with slices of beetroot. Aunt Nell prepared a fine fricassee of partridges. I made the pastry for a tart of codlin apples and Maggie churned cream and shelled peas. She started the raspberry jelly which Aunt Nell finished while Maggie polished the cutlery and set the table. Thank Heaven Papa does not entertain more often.

I think I must wed a rich man and have a kitchen full

of servants of which one shall be an excellent cook. I shall be glad when my birthday comes and I am fourteen, for then Papa will include me at dinner and I can wear my best silk with the beaded collar. But after the meal we shall all have to sing and Master Ruddiard says I am not yet ready for that. (He will never know how little I practise.)

On his arrival, Master Waybold told Papa that the plague has been caused by earthquakes in a distant part of the world. Apparently earthquakes allow pestilential seeds to rise from below the ground. These are then borne on the winds and carried to all parts of the world to cause sickness and death. Aunt Nell declared that if this is so 'tis no accident but the will of God. For my part I am sick to my teeth of reasons for the plague. What difference does it make how it came about?

I shall creep out now to the top of the stairs and see what else I can hear. At times I envy the menfolk. They have interesting lives which are denied to many women. Had I been born a boy I might have become a physician or a lawyer. Instead I shall be a wife and mother. I shall have to wed a man whose work I can discuss with him.

Later

There was much talk about the laxity of the authorities with regard to the possibility of plague. Master Waybold insists that there has been no provision for grain and meal to be stored and no public funds for relief of the poor. Papa blames the magistrates. Master Waybold blames the Lord Mayor. Apparently the French and Italians do things better. They put measures in place and regulations to prevent the possible spread of infection.

They then fell to discussing the new dances, many of which are French. New tunes are available, they say, for sarabands and jigs. Papa insisted that he prefers the English dances which are more elegant and less rowdy. But at his age I daresay he would. After my birthday I shall persuade Aunt Nell to ask Papa to find me a dancing tutor. He surely cannot refuse me indefinitely. I am no longer a child and if he wants me to find a good husband he must see that I have all the ladylike skills.

33

Saturday

I think 'tis the 18th — I am so confused I cannot think clearly. Such a dreadful thing happened this morning. I was leaving the house to visit Mistress Capperly when a young matron approached on the other side of the road. Of a sudden I heard a commotion and running footsteps behind me and I saw the woman's expression change to one of horror. I turned in alarm as a man passed me. He was stumbling, dirty and unkempt. He sang snatches of a most bawdy song and uttered the most horrible profanities. I shrank back against the wall but he paid me no heed. Instead, he took hold of the woman and, against her will, kissed her full on the mouth. I felt sick to see such a disgusting thing.

"Now you too will die of the plague!" he told her and stumbled on, laughing.

The young woman gazed at me with such horror in her eyes that I could not ignore her. Senseless with fear, she swayed and I stepped forward and caught her as she fell. I recognized the folly of it as soon as I held her in my arms and screamed for Aunt Nell who ran out to help me. Poppet ran out also but we paid him no heed. We dared not invite

34

her into the house but sat her against the wall outside. Aunt Nell sent me in for a mug of lemonade and we brought her round. Poppet then crept closer to her, whining softly, and she patted his head with a trembling hand. She could scarcely speak but whispered that her name was Madeline Gratton and she was on her way home from going to the apothecary to buy oil of cloves for her husband's toothache. In desperation she rubbed repeatedly at her mouth until Aunt Nell brought her a bowl of vinegar water and a face cloth to wipe away all trace of the man's vile kiss. All the while Poppet lay with his head in her lap and seemed besotted with her. I confess I felt a little jealous of this small betrayal but told myself that if he was of comfort to the poor soul I should be glad.

"That wretched man lied," I told Mistress Gratton with as much conviction as I could muster. "He was as healthy as you or I. His looks were more those of a drunkard. Believe me, 'twas nothing more than a cruel prank."

The poor creature shook her head. "He had the plague. I smelled it on him."

I thought it very likely but feared she would die of anxiety before the plague could claim her. We could not reassure her and later, with heavy hearts, watched her go on her way. Aunt Nell would not carry the vinegar water back into the house but emptied it into the gutter. Once inside the house she scoured the bowl with sand and threw the face cloth on to the fire to be rid of it. Her lips were closed tight and her hands trembled. In truth we were both badly shaken by the encounter. I wish I had been a mile away when the incident happened. 'Twas the nearest we have come to the pestilence and I shall not sleep tonight for thinking of it.

What a mournful noise the bells make. There are so many dead that they are tolled almost incessantly, reminding us constantly of the danger and our own fragility.

June 20th

In bed with griping pains in my stomach. Aunt Nell says I ate too well of the cherries Mistress Capperly sent round yesterday. (She has friends south of the Thames near Maidstone — Mistress Capperly, not Aunt Nell.)

June 23rd

A mighty bad start to the day. I took Poppet for a walk and saw a man throw himself under the wheels of a carriage. I knew 'twas no accident for I saw him wait until the last moment to hurl himself forward. The horses reared up and the carriage threatened to overturn but the driver brought it under control. Poppet barked himself hoarse and I confess I lingered to see how it would all end. The man was dazed and bleeding but not yet dead as a crowd gathered. Then a woman came running and said she was his wife.

It seemed their only son, who was a sailor on the *Royal Oak,* had died during the battle with the Dutch some weeks ago. Her husband, a prey to melancholy humours, had taken it very hard and had lost the will to live. The man was lifted up and carried to his home with the poor wife weeping beside him. I cut short Poppet's walk and returned home chastened by the sad spectacle.

June 24th

Another letter from Uncle John urging us all to leave London. He says the plague is taking a firm hold and we should leave while we can. According to rumours, if the plague becomes too bad Woolwich and the other villages will refuse entry to Londoners. Aunt Nell wants me to go but I begged Papa to let me stay, saying that perhaps the worst of the plague is over. I squeezed out a few tears and he relented "for the present." Aunt Mary sends her love and says we should chew a mixture of garlic and rosemary at all times to keep our lungs clear. It sounds most unpleasant and fortunately Papa thinks so too.

'Tis said that the bells will stop tolling next month by decree of the Lord Mayor and Aldermen. I wonder. London is abuzz with rumours and we no longer know what to believe.

June 25th

Lordsday. To church again but the congregation much smaller than before. The sermon was about sin and the punishments thereof. It seems likely that the plague is brought upon us by the iniquities of the population — a horrid notion. Papa was uneasy and wonders again if we should stay away from all public places until the plague is ended. 'Tis true we can say our prayers at home but for myself I should miss the meeting of friends and acquaintances and the thought of our empty pew saddens me.

June 26th

Monday. Or should I say Black Monday? Aunt Nell has a sick stomach and Maggie was sent in search of asses' milk for her but could find none. Mistress Capperly called in today to tell us not to go near St Giles where many are sick of the plague and most of those stricken are dying.

"The contagion is in the air everywhere," she insisted. "We should carry posies of sweet-smelling herbs to hold beneath our noses."

A curse on those countries abroad for sending us this plague.

Master Cox, the pie man, has not passed and I do recall he comes from the St Giles area. Has he been stricken? I hope not for he has a wife and two small children.

June 28th

Another hot day with scarcely any breeze. I found it impossible to sleep when I came to bed. Just after the stroke of twelve I heard a commotion in the street and crept to the window. I saw a man rolling on the cobbles, shrieking in agony. He tore at his collar, tearing the lace and screamed that devils were tormenting him.

He cried, "Get away from me, you hideous fiends!" and lashed out with his fists as though fighting invisible adversaries.

The link man arrived with his lantern and bent over the poor wretch. At once he recoiled from the man. He shouted, " 'Tis the plague!" in a most terrible voice and jumped back in a panic. Around me windows were flung open and heads

40

poked out. Mistress Capperly cried that the poor wretch was obviously delirious — a sure sign of the infection. Then Papa rushed into my room and slammed my window shut.

"You foolish child! Don't you know the contagion travels in the air?" Aunt Nell joined us and we watched as a blanket was thrown from a window and the unfortunate wretch was wrapped up in it and carried away.

"Is he dead?" someone asked the linkman.

"As good as!" was the reply. "They will take him to the pest house."

The man who lives opposite says plague was foretold back in March. It seems that on one fateful day the winds blew from both north and south at the same time and this is a sure sign.

June 29th

Mistress Capperly left London today. She took her ginger cat with her in a wicker basket and piled bags and boxes into a cart. The driver was a cheerful young man in his twenties who seemed happy to talk to me. His name is Luke and he told me that he has hired a cart and is earning good money taking folk into the countryside. He was an actor by profession

41

but audiences are thin. The theatres will soon all be closed. Maggie came out and tossed her yellow curls at him. I asked her loudly how her sweetheart, Jon, was faring in his wherry on the river. She threw me a poisonous look, flounced back into the house and banged the door behind her. I wonder if Luke has a sweetheart. Not that Papa would allow me to wed an actor. In his eyes they are all rogues and vagabonds. Why are parents so full of prejudice? I trust I shall keep an open mind when I am a parent.

It was quite a sight to see Mistress Capperly sitting atop her bundles as the horse set off at a comfortable pace. By that I mean he ambled along despite Luke's best efforts to hurry him. Mistress Capperly has a friend in Dorking who will accommodate her until the plague ends.

June 30th

The heat is intolerable. Aunt Nell is fidgety and bad tempered and has a pain in her head. As soon as I heard her speak of it I fell prey to a deep anxiety. What if our connection with Madeline Gratton has brought this about? I will write it plain — by that I mean THE PLAGUE. If so, I will hold myself responsible for 'twas I who called Aunt Nell into the street to help me.

42

July 1st

Another hot airless day. If only it would rain. Some of the pestilence might be washed away.

Shelling peas, I sat in the yard in the shade with my petticoats round my knees but still found little comfort.

Just before dark I heard a cat wailing in the street and there was Mistress Capperly's ginger cat. He'd escaped his basket and found his way home. I begged a few scraps of cold mutton and fed him on the doorstep. Poppet barked his head off. He was jealous, poor sweet.

July 3rd

Aunt Nell came home from the market looking very pale. She overheard two men discussing the Weekly Bills of Mortality. It seems that in the past week 700 people have died from the plague. So the plague is well and truly come to London after all. After much discussion I am to be sent to Woolwich with Aunt Nell. I refused to go without Poppet and Papa has relented. At least Poppet will enjoy the farm. Plenty of chickens to chase. I was sent to enquire of a carrier but was soon stopped in my tracks. One of the houses in the next street had a red cross painted on the door. Above the cross someone had chalked "Lord Have Mercy Upon Us."

The door had been padlocked on the outside and a man was sitting on the steps. He looked dirty and his clothes were tattered. He said he was the official watchman and that the house was "shut up." Inside was someone dying of the plague and nobody was allowed in or out.

"But how will they eat?" I asked.

"I'll run their errands." He grinned and I saw his horrid teeth. "For a small sweetener!" He rubbed his finger and thumb together and of a sudden I was glad to be going to Woolwich. But I could find no carriers for hire — they were all spoken for. Returned home deeply disturbed.

July 4th

Young Will came to the door today tho' we dared not let him in. Apart from his thievery there is plague in St Giles.

44

I was grating cheese for a rarebit. Will was as pert as ever and full of his usual tricks. Aunt Nell was still abed, still out of sorts. I took her some porridge but she couldn't keep it down. We gave Will some ham and a chunk of bread which he gobbled noisily, stuffing it in with his fingers. He said he had had great sport, following the cart.

"Which cart is that?" Maggie asked, looking in the larder for some milk.

"Why, the dead cart," he replied. "Every night as soon as 'tis dark it comes round to collect the dead."

I stared at him, my heart in my mouth. Then a shudder ran through me. Had it come to this?

Maggie clipped his ear and told him not to tell lies.

"But 'tis true," he insisted. "The graveyards are full up. Dead bodies on top of dead bodies." He pinched his nose and rolled his eyes. "And most of the gravediggers are fled into the country. They take the bodies to a pit now and tip them in. Higgledy, piggledy. All arms and legs. 'Tis a most gruesome sight."

Maggie said, "You lie, Will."

" 'Tis the truth," he insisted. "Half of the bodies are naked as the day they was born. Cross my heart and hope to—"

Maggie clapped a hand across his mouth. She gave him a slice of lemon tart to keep him quiet and we looked at each other.

"Then God is truly punishing us," Maggie cried. "We are

45

all going to die," and of a sudden burst into tears. We threw our arms around each other in fear and for a long moment clung together weeping. When we separated, young Will had disappeared taking with him the rest of the lemon tart as well as the cheese grater.

July 5th

Wednesday morning. I am writing this before I rise for breakfast. Yesterday a letter was handed in the door from a man who leaped back as soon as the door was opened. He asked querulously if we "had it in the house." By this he meant the plague. He was not at all reassured by my denial but scurried away leaving us to read the letter. It was from Master Ruddiard, to tell us he was leaving London with his parents to stay in East Grinstead until the plague was gone out of the City. He urged us to do the same and asked God to bless us. So — no more singing lessons. Life is changing in so many ways.

A letter is come too from Uncle John who tells us of a recipe for "Doctor Butler's Cordial Water" — a sure cure for the plague. It will drive all venom from the heart. It calls for half a pound of Venice treacle (which is nowhere to be

46

had in these days of sickness) as well as pimpernel, cardous, scordium and scabious. And rosewater for distillation. A month since we might have purchased all or some but now there are few medicaments to be had.

Papa asked the doctor to call because Aunt Nell is no better. When the doctor came he was like a stranger, so haggard and pale I scarcely knew him. He held a cloth soaked in vinegar to his mouth to keep out the contagion. He stayed for no more than a minute but I daresay we are fortunate he came at all. Many doctors have fled into the countryside with their families. Aunt Nell has a "high fever." He scribbled a list of medicaments for me to fetch from the apothecary.

On the doorstep he paused and whispered, "Get out of London before 'tis too late."

I hastened willingly to our nearest apothecary. It smells so exotic — scented as it is with a myriad of herbs. Dried mint, aniseed, cloves and ginger . . . the list is endless. Ever since I was child I have found the apothecary's a place of wonder with the sparkling array of coloured bottles, jars of every shape and size and stone jars tightly corked. Dried herbs hang from the ceiling, and baskets and boxes of sandalwood are piled on every counter. Everything is labelled, the contents noted in spidery Latin. Our apothecary looks as ancient as some of his ingredients with a leathery face and kindly blue eyes. Aunt Nell claims that he has been there since the beginning of time, his life prolonged by his own remedies.

47

I returned with what few medicaments I could buy. Pray God they will work their usual magic.

July 6th

I cannot write. My heart is too heavy. Maggie's mother is taken with the plague and will most likely die. As soon as Will told her, Maggie ran off to reach home before they are shut up. Aunt Nell is very angry and Papa muttered that servants no longer know where their loyalties lie. But I understand. Blood is stronger than water.

July 7th

At last we have seen the coal carrier. He brought us a hod full of coal and has promised another in two days' time. If he is spared that long, he added, crossing himself. He showed me a charm "To Repel The Distemper" which he has lately bought from a fortune-teller. It is a scrap of paper with the letters of the word ABRACADABRA writ in the form of an upturned triangle. At the bottom is an A, above that AB, above that ABR and so on until the whole word is done. The poor man knows nothing of the alphabet but still insists that this will protect him. I had no heart to tell him otherwise tho' I fear 'tis quite useless.

Without Maggie 'twas my job to venture into the other end of the attic to select a couple of pigeons for tonight's supper. How I hate that pigeon loft. A smelly, messy place but the pigeons seem happy enough. I took down the first two birds I could catch and took them to Aunt Nell in her sickbed. She eyed them askance.

"Old birds," she whispered. "Hardly worth cooking. Look at the legs, Alice. Young birds have pink legs. Go up and find some that are younger."

I said I could not bear to venture up there again and poor Aunt Nell had no energy to argue with me.

July 8th

I never thought to write such terrible words in this diary but tragedy has befallen us with a vengeance. Yesterday, when the doctor returned to see his patient, he told me that Aunt Nell's fever has not been broken. Of a certainty she has the plague. The disease must run its course, he warned. She may die. If tokens appear on her skin there is no hope for her. I stared at him, chilled from head to toe with a fear like nothing I have ever known. I tried to speak but the words eluded me. I felt dizzy and had to sit down. He said the house must be shut up so that we do not go out and infect others.

"Not the plague!" I whispered, when I at last found my voice. " 'Tis the spotted fever, surely?"

He shook his head wearily and wrote out a prescription. Back I went to the apothecary for more medicaments. On the way home I fell into the most fearful panic and I was sorely tempted to run away. The thought of being locked in with a victim of the plague made me tremble. I feared I would fall to the ground in a swoon like poor Mistress Gratton. Then I came to my senses and was truly ashamed of my cowardice. How could I think of abandoning my aunt? Aunt Nell, who had been a mother to me all these years. Regardless of passers-by, I sank to my knees and prayed for courage for the ordeal ahead of me. God heard my prayer and I came home with a heavy heart.

Within the hour the doors were barred front and back and I was under strict orders not to open the lower windows for fear the contagion leaks out into the street and infects passers-by. A watchman has been appointed to help us. He is clean enough but seems a little too fond of his jug of ale. He sprawls against the door, half asleep, clutching the jug to him. I cannot say I like him but he is not disrespectful — yet.

By the time Papa returned from work he found himself locked out and nothing would persuade the watchman to let him in. Once in Papa would be unable to go out again. On second thoughts he felt he could be more help outside than in. We decided he should lodge with one of his colleagues if he could find anyone willing to accommodate him. Perhaps Master Waybold would oblige. He left us, vowing to return on the morrow to help in any way he could.

July 9th

I stared at myself in the mirror this morning and saw a frightened stranger. Aunt Nell lay in the next room. I had washed her face and hands but dared go no further for fear of doing her some harm. Already there is a cruel swelling in her neck — the beginning of a bubo which will cause her much pain. I tell myself she will survive and cling to this thought. Just before three I heard the door being unlocked and hurried down the stairs full of hope. A frightful apparition waited at the foot of the stairs. I screamed with shock but as soon as it spoke I knew it was the doctor.

"My newly issued protective garment," he told me in

51

muffled tones. "Hot and cumbersome but 'twill keep out the contagion."

It was the strangest apparel I have ever seen in my life. A long loose garment covered him entirely with the exception of his head. It was made all of soft thin leather and I saw at once that with the July heat he would roast within it. The headpiece was a leather helmet with a beaklike nose and eyepieces of thin horn that he could see through. I pitied him with all my heart. Who would wish to be a doctor when plague strikes the city?

I led him upstairs into my aunt's chamber.

"I fear she is delirious this morning," I told him. "She doesn't know me."

" 'Tis a common symptom," he told me. "If she recovers it will pass."

He was tender with Aunt Nell as he examined her. I caught another glimpse of the bubo, which was a small purple swelling, then stepped back a pace. Aunt Nell's confusion was obvious yet the doctor's strange garment aroused no comment.

"You are home early tonight," she murmured, thinking the voice was Papa's. "Supper will be ready shortly."

The doctor shook his head in answer to my unspoken question.

"We can do little for her," he told me. "The sickness must run its course. If the bubo breaks open she has a chance. It will release the poison."

If it does not, then she will surely die.

And so will I, I thought but kept that to myself. Tonight I have tried to make a pact with God.

"Dear God in Heaven, if you will preserve us all, including Poppet, I promise I will never say an unkind word again. Nor will I be hasty or lazy. *Please* God, hear my prayer . . . I will pray twice a day and be charitable towards the poor — as soon as I have married well. I will try harder with my pastry and practise my singing. I will spend more time with Maggie at her writing lessons and I will crochet a hundred collars."

But doubtless God is being overwhelmed with such entreaties. Will he even hear mine among the clamour? Has he heard Maggie's prayers for her mother, I wonder?

Papa called by to say that Master and Mistress Waybold have gone to her sister's house in Chatham and that he is staying in the house they have left empty. His presence, they trust, will deter robbers who grow ever more daring as the plague increases. They prey on the sick and steal from abandoned houses.

July 10th

The doctor says Aunt Nell is no better and no worse. He tells me that the King's Court has moved upriver to

53

Hampton Court. The Parliament will next assemble in Oxford in October.

"So we are abandoned to our fate," I said with some bitterness.

"Not so," he replied. "We have our own Lord Mayor and Aldermen. We shall be well served."

I hope he is right. I am so tired but am managing better than I expected. When I need food I lower a basket on a rope from the upper window. There is money in it and I tell the watchman what we need. He sets off, still clutching his jug, and brings back the goods when he can find them. (I notice he always steals a few coins for his trouble but the poor wretch has to live.) Then I draw the basket up again. I have almost forgotten how life was before this disaster overtook us.

I am keeping busy. I have lit a fire in Aunt Nell's chamber and each day steep rosemary leaves in vinegar. Then I toss the liquid on to the hot coals which send out much vapour to fumigate the air she breathes. The window is then opened and the stale contagious air is driven out.

Today I washed Aunt Nell tho' it turned my stomach to do so. She was never robust but now she is almost wasted away and her arms and legs no more than sticks. I forced myself to lay the soapy face cloth upon her body. I tried to avert my eyes for it seemed an impertinence to see her without her clothes but at last I overcame my unease. The swelling grows daily in size and is coming to a head. 'Tis full of loathsome matter but

54

this will be discharged when it breaks. If it does. Her skin is hot to the touch with fever, her lips chapped and split.

Poor dear Aunt Nell. The terrible pain makes her scream in agony and has affected her mind. She often calls me "Mother." Perhaps she thinks she is a child again. Once today she gave a little smile. I wanted tell her that I loved her but the words would not come. Have I ever told her?

July 11th

I am still unused to the growing silence. There are fewer bells being rung this month since the constant tolling was depressing the townsfolk. The dead are buried mostly at night and in silence which is almost more depressing than the bells. I keep recalling what Maggie's young brother told us of the dead cart and the burial pit. I have made myself a promise that if Aunt Nell dies I will not allow her to suffer such indignities.

I was cheered today by the appearance of Will, sent by Maggie to see how we are faring. It seems he went missing when the padlocks were put on their doors. I think he is better off roaming the streets than locked in with the plague. With his cap on at a rakish angle, he stood in the middle of the street, staring up at the window. He told me that his little sister has the plague and

55

that his mother has died and gone to Heaven with the angels. All this in such a cheery voice that I cannot help but smile.

"Ma will like it there," he said. "She likes to sing hymns and they all have lovely white wings so they can fly around the sky. And white clothes. I asked Maggie who will do their washing but she says it will all be seen to. All very proper."

He said also that charitable folk all over England are sending money to help the London poor at this time of great sickness and distress. Thousands of pounds, he told me, adding that when they receive their share of it they will surely be rich. I did not care to disillusion him tho' I have heard a similar rumour.

I told him I had nothing for him but he said he had something for me. With a sober expression he produced the cheese grater from behind his back. Hiding my amusement, I lowered my basket and he tossed the grater in.

"Because Ma can see me now," he confided.

I wonder if my mother can see me. If she can she will surely help me through this fearful time.

July 12th

Poor Poppet is getting very naughty but I cannot chide him. He hates to be confined all day and scratches the back door, hoping to be allowed into the yard. How can I tell him it is barred on the outside? He needs exercise, poor creature.

July 13th

This morning I was alerted by a stone thrown against the chamber window and looked out to see Luke in the street below. He was sitting on the seat of his cart holding the reins of his horse — a bay like the horse I rode in Woolwich not so long ago. He had come by, he said, to satisfy himself that I was still alive.

"You see that I am, Master Luke," I said. "Locked up and alone but still in the land of the living."

He asked if he could help in any way and I told him that I had not seen my father for three days. He promised to make enquiries when he had time but was on his way to collect a family from Cheapside who were fleeing into Essex to camp out on the marshes. I told him that when I could escape my home I would make my way to Woolwich.

"If anyone will give you passage," he said, his manner at once sober. "I hear you will need a Bill of Health. There are hundreds waiting at The Old Bailey for the precious scrap of paper. But to get it you will need a letter signed by your doctor."

He looked so healthy and cheerful that despite his gloomy words he lifted my spirits entirely and I found myself more cheerful for his visit.

When the doctor called he said the bubo must be brought to a head by hot poultices and asked if he should send in a nursewoman. I rejected the idea saying that I would do it. Under his guidance I prepared the poultice. Bread was soaked in boiling water, squeezed almost dry and wrapped in a cloth. This was applied directly to the swelling but my poor aunt screamed so loudly in such agony that I was overcome by fright and fainted clean away.

When I came to my senses I felt blood oozing from a gash on my forehead. The doctor told me I had struck my head on the corner of the chest. I was in such a state that the doctor insisted I could not try again with my aunt's poultice. He will send in a nursewoman by the name of Mistress Sweet who has some experience of the work.

July 14th

Each day is worse than the one before it. I have doubled my prayers but God has turned his face from us. Today Mistress Sweet, the nursewoman, arrived. She is a filthy, ungainly creature who smokes a clay pipe at all times. I swear her long, straggly hair has never seen a comb nor has she discovered what wonders a wash cloth and soap will do for dirty skin. The clay pipe, she insists, keeps her lungs safe. I wonder what she uses for tobacco for the smoke is disgusting. She wears no protective clothing and yet seems to be untouched by the contagion. Aunt Nell would never allow such a foulmouthed woman into the house if she were well but what can I do but abide by the doctor's wishes?

Aunt Nell asked once for food and I gave her all that we have — a slice of bread and a pickled egg which, poor soul, she could not eat and shrieked that I was trying to poison her. Tomorrow I will fetch and pluck one of the few remaining pigeons and make a thin broth. Maybe she will be able to take some of that.

I could not bear to be present while the poultice was applied but I heard my aunt scream and knew the work was done. I was thanking God that the worst was over when, of a sudden, the door of her bedchamber was thrown open. Somehow Aunt Nell had found the strength to walk. She staggered past me to the top of the stairs. There was a kind of madness about her and her eyes rolled unseeing in her head.

She cried, "Your damned cures will be the death of me."

I was truly shocked for Aunt Nell never uses bad language. Before I could steady her she lost her footing and plunged headfirst down the stairs. She landed at the

59

bottom with a leg twisted beneath her and lay as still as death. I made haste to help her.

"Help me lift her," I begged the nursewoman who watched from above. The accursed wretch shook her shaggy head.

"I've done all I'm paid to do," she told me, wiping podgy hands on her dirty apron. "That bubo's hard as a rock. 'Tis never going to break. I've seen 'em like that before. But the fall's most likely killed her."

Clinging to the handrope, she lumbered down the stairs, shouting to the watchman to unlock the door and let her out.

"Go then and good riddance!" I cried, for suddenly I longed to be rid of her. The thought of her careless hands touching my aunt angered me.

"She is never to be allowed back in," I told the watchman.

So much for Mistress Sweet, I thought bitterly as the door slammed behind her. Sweet by name but not by nature.

One step at a time I pulled and tugged my aunt upstairs — she was skin and bone and light as a kitten — and laid her on the bed. She was so still. Her eyes were closed but when I spoke to her she mumbled something. I gasped with relief for I had believed her dead. I wiped her face with a damp cloth and made her as comfortable as I could. I pulled the sheet up to her chin and sat beside her until she slipped into a deep sleep. I lifted her right arm to tuck it beneath the sheet and received a most grievous shock. Dark marks were visible below the skin.

60

Plague tokens. I was so shocked that my heart raced.

So much for my prayers, I thought. Aunt Nell is going to die and the fault is mine. How can I live with such terrible guilt?

July 15th

Aunt Nell is dead. Pray God she is with my mother in Heaven. I am weak from weeping and can write no more today.

July 16th

I cannot believe Aunt Nell is gone from us. Nor will I ever forget the actual manner of her passing. Yesterday I went into her room as soon as I woke and was astonished to find her sitting upright in the bed. Her gaze was clear as she looked at me.

"Alice, my dear, I would like a pear," she said.

The words were so clear and she looked so much recovered that of a sudden I was filled with a most desperate hope. Unable to speak a word I simply stared at her, my heart thumping. There was a touch of colour in her face and her eyes were bright, with no sign of confusion.

"A pear?" I stammered. "Yes, yes. You shall have one."

A pear? But how at a time like this could I come by such a thing?

She nodded. "A sweet, juicy pear."

Could I send the watchman in search of one? I knew there were none to be found in the stricken city but I had to try. Before I could speak she smiled and I blinked back tears. Here was my own Aunt Nell miraculously restored to me. I fell to my knees beside the bed and took her hand in mine.

She sank back against the pillows and gave a long sigh. Still smiling, she whispered, "Letty, my dear!" Then she closed her eyes.

For a long while I could not move but waited for her to open her eyes and speak to me. Poppet came pattering into the room and jumped on the bed. He crept closer to her. He put his head on one side. Then his ears went down. I felt a cold chill. Could a dog know?

Was it all over? He whined softly, lay down beside her and with a little sigh, rested his head on his paws.

Later, when I was able, I washed Aunt Nell, sprinkled lavender water over her and dressed her in a clean nightgown. She looked very peaceful. I wrote to Papa and sent the

62

watchman off with the letter. I gave him money to buy some flowers if he could find any.

"Roses," I told him, "for they were her favourites."

Hours have passed and he has not returned.

When the doctor called I asked that my aunt be buried next to my mother but he says there are no spaces left in the graveyards and few to do the burying. So I must after all surrender her body to the dead cart. The idea was hateful to me but I could see no other way.

It was gone eleven that night when the cart came by. I heard the mournful cry — "Bring out your dead!" long before it reached our door. 'Twas smaller than I expected and pulled by a tired looking donkey. The watchman unlocked the door and the driver helped me carry Aunt Nell. Five or six other unfortunates were already laid side by side. Not higgledy-piggledy as I had feared, but as neat as possible. 'Tis true two were naked but three were dressed in a variety of garments. The last was wrapped in a tattered blanket. I had wrapped Aunt Nell in a clean sheet so that none would look upon her.

"I would like to go with her," I told the driver. "To see her to her last resting place."

The man shook his head. "I've heard that a hundred times or more," he told me in a kindly voice. " 'Tis clear against the rules. You have to stay shut up in your house."

"I have money—"

63

"Don't try to bribe me. Would you have me end my days in the Fleet Prison?"

As the cart trundled away I said the Lord's Prayer then hid my face in my hands. I heard the rattle of wheels and the wheezing of the donkey and once again the plaintive cry rang out.

"Bring out your dead!"

I wondered how many others would surrender the bodies of dead loved ones that night. How many other poor souls would join my aunt in the cart and be tossed into a hastily-dug pit. I did not open my eyes until the mournful sounds had finally faded. I think the sound of wheels on cobbles will haunt me for the rest of my life.

Later

I have killed Aunt Nell. The dreadful thought will not leave me. I would do anything to turn back the clock. If I could, I would leave poor Mistress Gratton to her fate and save my aunt. My own flesh and blood has been sacrificed for a stranger. How can I bear it? If only I could talk with Papa he might find a way to ease this terrible guilt. But he does not come and I wonder if he, too, is stricken. I have started to crochet another collar. It will be my penance.

64

July 17th

I am quite alone now except for Poppet. Young Will came by with four eggs. He would not say how he came by them and I was reluctant to ask. Food is so scarce. The woman with the cow no longer passes us and there are precious few vegetables to be had. And certainly no fruit. If only I had been able to grant Aunt Nell her last request for a juicy pear. But I must not complain. There are loaves aplenty by order of the authorities and they will not let the bakers overcharge us. I am becoming thankful for small mercies.

I am using my first collar as a pattern and have managed two neat rows, tho' I shed so many tears over it, I fear it may shrink before 'tis done.

July 18th

It seems that last week more than 1,000 folk died in London. The watchman has returned with the gloomy news. He

65

has brought no flowers and pretends he was robbed of the money I gave him. Still, he is someone to talk to and I am horribly lonely.

"A thousand?" I asked. "But not all dead of the plague, surely."

The wretch shrugged.

"Some are dead from other causes," I insisted. "Consumption, dropsy, jaundice . . . scurvy, of course, and accidents . . . And — and infants who died at birth." I wondered how many had died of grief or, bowed down by guilt or sorrow, had taken their own lives.

The watchman shrugged again and would not look up at me. 'Tis like talking to a stone at times.

"Either way they're dead!" he muttered and drank deeply from his jug.

I slammed the window on the stupid creature.

July 19th

I try not to think about Aunt Nell and her sad end. Papa will be desolate when he gets my letter and I miss her most dreadfully. Still no news of Papa and today the watchman has disappeared again. There is no one to fetch food for me but the doctor may look in on me if he passes this way.

66

July 21st

Poppet has run away. I feared this would happen. The poor pet was so desperate to get out of the house he leaped from the upper window. Mercifully he seemed unharmed by the fall and scampered off, barking joyfully and revelling in his freedom. Now I fear the dog-catcher will take him. Without him the house is silent but at least I am still free of any plague symptoms. Has God heeded my prayers? If he has then I cannot impose on him further to find my dog.

The collar is growing slowly and is very neat.

The weather continues close and mighty hot. We need a cool breeze or a refreshing shower.

July 22nd

Praise be for young Will. He called by with three oranges and a note from Maggie. I pulled it up and dried it between two flat stones heated in the fire to rid it of the contagion. When I thought it safe I unfolded it. Maggie prays the worst is over for her family — no more having taken the sickness. Young Will is on his way to see how Jon Ruddle fares. I wanted to ask Will to go in search of Poppet but he ran off before I could do so. Determined not to lose my dog to the dog-catcher I hailed a young woman who was passing the house with a posy of herbs held to her nose. I promised her a silver pin as a reward if she could find Poppet.

"A King Charles spaniel," I said. "And handsome. Brown and white with a smudge of black over his left eye."

She was deliberating what to make of this offer when a commotion arose and, as if on cue, Poppet himself appeared round the corner of the street. My delight turned to horror, for he was pursued by the dog-catcher, noose in hand. The latter was ugly, red-faced and angry. He called my sweet dog "a mangy cur" and made a snatch at him. Poor Poppet scrabbled at our front door begging to be let in and I shouted at the dog-catcher not to harm him.

By this time, the young woman had hastened away. Who can blame her? We made such a racket between us. I was screaming and Poppet was barking. The dog-catcher was uttering the most beastly oaths as he tried to grab Poppet's collar. At last the wretch had Poppet by the collar and held him up to show me.

"A quick twist of the neck . . ." he muttered, leering up at me with a most foul expression.

"Spare him!" I begged but his answer was to fasten both hands around Poppet's neck.

In a moment I had Aunt Nell's purse in my hand and was holding up a shilling. "Put the dog in my basket and this shall be yours," I told him.

I doubted he would earn that much in a normal month but the wretch laughed scornfully.

"Is he worth so little then?" he demanded.

I dared not give him all the money in the purse for how should I buy food when it was empty? Poppet was squealing with fright and I could not bear it. Within moments he might be dead, dangling from the man's hands. I snatched off my ring and held it up.

"This ring, then?"

"The shilling *and* the ring for your mangy cur!"

His greed sickened me. I think his cunning face and sly eyes will haunt my dreams. I shook my head. He then began to insist that I throw down the shilling before he would release the dog. I gambled on his greed and held my ground and he at last relented. But worse was to come. As I began to draw up the basket. Poppet leaped out and made to scamper off again. My heart raced for fear that I should lose him after all. But the dog-catcher wanted his reward and caught him again. Seconds later Poppet was in my arms and I was weeping for joy.

69

For a brief moment I was tempted to deny the fellow the shilling but thought better of it. If Poppet escaped again, he might forswear his ill-gotten gains and kill him out of spite.

Instead I tossed the shilling over his head so that he missed it. I took some small pleasure in watching him scramble among the grassy cobbles. Damn him for a scoundrel.

Not knowing what Poppet had been doing, I gave him a bath to rid him of any contagion that might linger in his fur. He made a great fuss and splashed water everywhere. It used up much of my remaining soap but I thought it well spent.

July 23rd

I watch my little dog with hawk-like eyes for fear he will escape again. This morning I considered my finances. The money from Aunt Nell's purse was almost gone but I still had the ring and I could sell Papa's best pewter bowl if necessary. There was also Aunt Nell's jewellery.

Watching this morning from the upper window I saw three rats in the street below. Never so bold before, I fear that the plague regulations are to blame. There are so few dogs and cats left to deal with the rats that the horrid creatures are

70

making hay, so to speak. I clapped my hands but they did not even run from the sound. Grass, now, is thick between the cobbles and a few weeds grow so that the street looks sadly neglected. 'Tis rare nowadays to see a fine horseman pass by. Anyone who can afford to flee London has gone long since.

I now appreciate all that made life beautiful before the plague came. Music, cheerful conversation, laughter. Not to mention good food and drink. I wonder if they will ever come again.

July 25th

The doctor, finding the door unattended and the key in the padlock, called in and was surprised to find me still unaffected by the plague. He suggests that I will not catch it now and eventually will be released from this prison. The quarantine period is 40 days so I shall be locked up until August 14th. Almost three more weeks. I told him I should be dead from hunger by then for I have no watchman. He promised to see that the wretch is replaced.

July 27th

Still no sign of the promised watchman but I am too unhappy to care. My head aches and I have stayed in my bed. The clock has just struck midday and I have eaten nothing all day and yesterday — nought but a lump of rancid cheese that any decent mouse would refuse.

Later

I was interrupted by a shout from below and there was young Will, his face alight with glee. Send down the basket, he tells me, and sends me up a veritable feast. Bread, a jar of pickled walnuts, a pot of plum jam and a flagon of ginger beer. It seems he has raided an abandoned house, taking from the larder whatever was to be found.

"I crept round the back and climbed in the window," he told me cheerfully. "Found the poor old beggar dead in his stinking bedchamber — and not a stitch on. Smothered in

72

tokens." He wrinkled his nose in disgust. "Not that he *was* a beggar. 'Twas a grand house so he must've been a rich man. I thought, what's he want with food, so I helped meself."

I know stealing is wrong but I could not scold him. Maggie is well, he says, and he provides food for the family. He utters this information with such pride. I pray God he is not arrested and thrown into the Fleet Prison. I shall never pass that place again without uttering a prayer for the unfortunate prisoners. I know only too well now what it means to be locked up — and at least I am in the comfort of my father's house.

After he had gone I ate my fill. Poppet would not touch the walnuts but licked some jam from a saucer and ate some bread. Then he curled up in his basket and fell to snoring. Even that sound is better than the silence.

July 28th

Felt queasy all day. Pain in my gut and some vomiting.

July 29th

The vomiting has ceased but I feel so tired. I can barely drag myself up and down the stairs. Surely the plague has not caught me at last? Poppet whines so and the constant whimpering irritates me. To my eternal shame I slapped him. His look was so reproachful that I at once gathered him into my arms and begged his forgiveness.

July 30th

No change. I sit and stare from the window and ponder on my life. I wonder if I will live to see my birthday on August 3rd.

July 31st

The doctor came again. Still melting within his special suit in the summer heat. He tells me 'tis not the plague (Heaven be praised) but most likely rancid cheese or too many pickled walnuts. They have aggravated my digestion. I hope I deserve such wonderful news. I thank my mother and Aunt Nell. I believe they must be looking down on me to preserve me from worse disasters.

The doctor has discovered that Papa is in the pesthouse in Old Street. So now I know why he has stopped calling here. Poor Papa. He was taken sick suddenly in the street and carried away in haste. He is hovering between life and death and I am unable to help him. Dear Papa. Forgive me for all my careless ways. If God spares you I will be a model daughter to you. What will he say when he learns of Aunt Nell's death?

August 3rd

My fourteenth birthday. I am well enough to make my way from bed to window. Outside 'tis still hot and humid. My new watchman has appeared at last. As wiry as a ferret with eyes like currants but he greets me cheerily with a wave of his hat. His name is Thomas Winn. He ran off on his errands and returned with two loaves (a most glorious sight) from the baker. Also eight potatoes and a jar of lemoncurd bought from a countrywoman in what remains of the market. He says there are daily less farmers willing to risk a visit to the city. Tomorrow he will try for fish at the river. Some of the watermen, now lacking fares, eke out their existence by fishing with rods. 'Tis a strange sight, he says, to see so few boats upon the Thames.

Two days later — I think

(I lose track of the days.) Last night I was awoken in the dead of night to hear Poppet scratching at the door of my bedchamber. I let him out and he flew down the stairs barking hysterically. I lit my candle and followed him with some caution and ended up in the kitchen where the window had been broken. A man was climbing out but Poppet leaped up and caught his ankle. The man screeched and kicked out and Poppet was thrown across the room. He landed on a stack of pans with a frightful clatter. He added his howls to the racket and Master Winn banged on the front door to ask what was happening. I was tempted to seize the man's foot but recalled the incident with Madeline Gratton. Instead I took up one of the fallen saucepans and hit him on the leg. He fell out of the window and disappeared.

With my heart beating fit to burst I picked up Poppet and ran upstairs. I opened the window and told Master Winn what had happened.

"Did he take anything?" he asked.

"Not to my knowledge," I told him, "but I will know better in the daylight."

He promised to send for a glazier on the morrow and we said our "Goodnights." I patted my little dog for his cleverness and slid between the sheets. I thought about the intruder but could not find it in my heart to wish him ill. Any man who breaks into a locked up house is risking the plague. The poor wretch must have been desperate. Another Will, I thought. Is our poor city brought to this?

August 6th

Only eight more days and I will be free. I am counting the hours. The doctor has promised me a letter of health. But first I must seek out the pesthouse in Old Street and ask after Papa. Please God he will survive.

Two or three days later

Master Winn is a most amiable young man. We have talked much these last few days. He is, or was, a wealthy merchant's servant but the family fled the City at the very outset. They left the two manservants and a maidservant to their fates. Despite this unkindness he is a cheerful soul. Yesterday he took some coins and went in search of food and brought back a rare treat. Oysters. I opened them, splashed them with a little vinegar and sent down half to him by way of a "Thank you" for his efforts.

He finally found a glazier but the man would not enter our house for fear of the plague. I have tacked a length of sacking across the kitchen window for want of something better.

Master Winn thinks today is August 10th

Only four more days. Then true freedom for me and for Poppet. What will he make of it, I wonder.

August 11th

Master Winn says there is a new decree — that fires must be lit in every street. In this terrible heat.

"Are they trying to kill off those who have so far survived?" I asked him.

"The fires are to burn the pestilence from the air," he replied.

It seems they are to be lit outside every twelfth house. The maintenance of the fire is to be shared by the six householders on either side who must provide the wood. Impossible, I told him. Half of us are prisoners. We have no way to earn money and have none to spend on firewood. I despair.

Poppet was very naughty today. He gnawed the leg of Papa's favourite chair. He never did such a thing even when he was a pup, but he is bored now and I have forgiven him. It is beyond repair but hopefully Papa will overlook it when — if — he returns. (I shall never take anything for granted again.)

August 13th

Half past eight has just struck and I must be up and about. I shall wash and dry my hair for the journey tomorrow. Then Poppet and I shall walk through the door and on to the street. I almost dread it now 'tis so near. What will the day bring? No more sorrow, I hope. Dare I make my way to Maggie's house to ask after her? I have not seen Will for some time and wonder why. But is venturing into that area a great risk? I will ask the doctor if he comes . . .

Six o'clock in the evening

I now have my precious letter. It reads thus.

This is to confirm that Alice Paynton has not succumbed to the plague and is of sound health. She has resided for 40 days and nights in the house in which her aunt died. She now wishes passage to Woolwich where she will join her uncle, one John Paynton, and his family.
Signed Andrew Wickham, Physician
14th August 1665

I shall take some food and drink in a basket. I will need money so will pawn Aunt Nell's opal brooch and Papa's leather-bound Bible. Then these may be redeemed when Papa returns and this nightmare is at an end. I shall also take my diary, a pen and a small bottle of ink.

August 15th

The sun is barely up but I can see to write and shall recount yesterday's adventure. I write this sitting up in my own bed having spent all of yesterday in the following ways.

I was up early and made my way with Poppet towards Old Street. A strange and fearful journey. I never thought to see the city so quiet and sombre. The streets are almost empty and those folk that venture out keep to themselves. The women hide their faces behind posies of herbs while some men prefer cloths wrapped around the face up to their eyes.

Poppet hardly knew what to make of it all and trotted beside me in a most subdued manner. We passed two dead cats which puzzled him and a small piglet running from an irate man whose language bears no repeating. Poppet perked up and would have given chase but I held tight to his lead, wrapping it once around my hand to shorten it. I was determined, should we meet a dog-catcher, that I would carry Poppet under my arm until we were safely past him.

When I reached Old Street I at once met with a defeat. The pesthouse was a dismal building but I marched right in, refusing to be cowed. The man at the desk listened to me with indifference. Finally he took out a clay pipe and filled and lit it. Paynton? The name meant nothing to him.

"But you must have a list," I insisted, coughing from the loathsome smoke. "You will find my father's name. Edmund Paynton."

Shaking his head, he sucked noisily at his pipe.

"He works for the Navy Board. He was brought—"

"He might work for King Charles himself — it makes little difference to me!"

I longed to shake him but somehow kept a civil tongue. "Then who can help me?"

He shrugged. The regular man, he said, had fallen sick and was admitted less than an hour since. I pitied that poor fellow with all my heart. I would not leave, however, until I had news of Papa. An hour passed. Poppet grew restless but at last a physician appeared and he produced a list of deaths. Finding a name among so many took more time and my heart raced with a frightful anxiety. But at last I heard the best news possible. That Papa was not among the dead. He will leave on the 4th September.

"You cannot visit him, but you can leave a note if you wish."

I tore a page from my diary and wrote that I was going to Woolwich. I decided the news of Aunt Nell's death must wait until he is stronger in mind and body.

I went home, weary to my bones and slept long and deep.

83

Today I shall go to the Old Bailey and collect my Certificate of Health. Then I must hire a horse or find a carter to take me to Uncle John's farm.

Time to get up.

Later

Another long and fretful day. The sun is setting and I am still at home. At least I have my precious certificate. The line of people outside the Old Bailey numbered a hundred or more when I arrived. I was struck at once by the number wearing mourning bands. Hardly a soul had not lost a loved one. It brought tears to my eyes to think on the grief this plague has brought upon the good people of London.

The clock struck ten as I took my place behind a large man with a ravaged face and eyes red from weeping. Turning to me, his first words were, "Can you read?"

When I nodded he thrust a letter into my hand. 'Twas written by a Doctor Molloy, confirming health and fitness. His face lightened with relief as I deciphered the spiky handwriting.

"I trust nobody," he muttered. Kissing the letter, he carefully refolded it.

Thinking to while away the time I tried to strike up a

conversation but he had no further use for me and kept his mouth resolutely shut.

I had left Poppet at home for fear he would grow restless or run off. No such thought had entered the head of the woman who took her place behind me in the fast growing line. She had brought a green parrot which chattered ceaselessly within its wicker cage. I realized that it uttered the most profane words. Perhaps my shock showed in my eyes for the woman gave me an anxious glance.

" 'Tis French the bird speaks," she told me.

"Indeed?" I said. "I know nothing of that language."

Which seemed to reassure her. She then told me with no prompting (she was a talkative soul) that she had spent five hours in the line yesterday only to be turned away when they closed. She was tenth in line by that time. Others had spent days trying to obtain their certificates. My heart sank. If I am out of luck today, I vowed, I must rise earlier tomorrow.

I told her of my loss and the miracle that I had not taken the disease. She, it seemed, had had the plague and recovered. Her mother, father and sister had all died. Her father's parrot was all that remained, she said, and she would not be parted from it.

"But God spared me!" Her eyes shone as she made the sign of the cross.

She told me she was determined to go to her brother who lives in Bromley and raises each year a vast flock of

85

geese. These he brings up to London each December for the Christmas trade — a journey taken on foot and lasting many days. The thought of these creatures waddling slowly towards their fate troubled me. But then I remembered the fine bird we had last Christmas with chestnut stuffing and bread sauce, and I hastily put the thought aside. I tried to imagine our next Christmas dinner and failed. With God's help Papa will be with us, but without Aunt Nell the celebration will be a sad affair. I brushed tears from my eyes as the guilt flooded in again. I had brought about my aunt's death and nothing could ever be the same again.

Just before six I was ushered inside the building and made my way to an ornate desk where the large man waited his turn, his fingers crossed behind his back. The clerk seated at the desk read his letter carefully and then he frowned.

He said, "Doctor Molloy? The name's unfamiliar."

I saw the large frame tremble as the man behind the desk scanned a sheaf of names.

"Where did you get this?" he asked. "We have no Molloy listed. This letter is a forgery. Worthless. How did you come by it?"

The man stared at him open-mouthed, seemingly struck silent by his dismay.

The clerk handed back the letter. "Whatever you paid for it, you have been cheated . . . Next!"

86

Until this day I had not seen a grown man weep as that man did but I could not pity him. Had he been fit a doctor would surely have confirmed it. So was he ill of the plague? I had stood behind him in the line for hours. Or was he still recovering? Had he broken out of a locked house? I drew back from him in a fright as he stumbled past me. He muttered incoherently beneath his breath, rubbing at his tears with his sleeve. The man behind the desk shook his head in despair.

"A rogue or a fool. The latter I pity. The gullible are easy prey for quacks," he told me as he searched his list for *my* doctor's name and finding it, nodded. He filled out a certificate, signed and sealed it. "Next!"

I smiled at the parrot lady as I left and we wished each other well. I came home and came to bed. Now my writing is done I shall pray most earnestly. I missed seeing Master Winn. Doubtless, now that he is no longer needed here, he is guarding another house somewhere in the city.

August 16th

It is half past six and I have decided to visit Maggie before I set off for Woolwich. I have been to her house once and

87

hope I may find it again. I cannot leave London without discovering how they fare. If I see Will I shall tell him of my flight to the country . . .

Seven o'clock the same evening

I ventured into St Giles with a posy of herbs at my nose and spoke with Maggie who was pleased to see me. She looks very tired but has so far survived. She, Will and one sister are all that remain of her family but Will is thrown into the Fleet Prison for stealing from an abandoned house. She begged me to enquire after him before I go.

"If the plague does not claim him he will die of gaol fever!" she insisted.

So, with no great liking for the errand, I set out for the prison. On reaching it I saw an iron grating through which a motley collection of arms waved. A small crowd had gathered and many conversations were taking place so that the noise was appalling. From further inside voices called for food in tones of great desperation. I entered the gate and found a warder — a scrawny man wearing clothes too big for him. He said he had no one there by that name.

"But he is here!" I insisted. "I have a message from his sister and must speak with him."

"Then ask for him outside."

I returned to the grating and fearfully pushed a way through the crowd. I asked for Will and after an interval his cheeky face appeared. He seemed not one whit dismayed by his situation and his grin was as broad as ever.

"Come to get me out, have you?" he asked.

Such a thought had never entered my head, but now it seemed I must try to help him. Not only for Maggie's sake but for the good he had done me. I owed him a favour. A young man said I would have to bribe the warder, so back I went. I found the wretch gnawing at a chicken leg. I suggested that Will might be released to make room in the prison for a more serious offender. The man laughed in my face. Seeing how few good teeth he had I wondered how he could eat the chicken. He asked what I should give him and I was stumped for an answer.

"A pewter flagon," I suggested. Papa would be angry but I would face that when it came.

He argued for more but I was adamant that we had nothing else. Tossing the chicken bone over his shoulder he wiped his mouth with the back of his hand and said, "Fetch it." I hurried home and took the smallest of the two flagons. Then I had a better idea. I took the flagon to a money lender who lent me two shillings on it. I told him I would repay the

89

money after the plague and he swore to keep it for me. When I reached the prison I offered the warder one of the shillings, saying I had sold the flagon for him. He held out his hand but I withdrew it.

"I want to see Will first."

He spat to show his disdain but went away. I heard his footsteps as he went down the stone steps and minutes later he returned with Will. As I held out the shilling Will snatched it from my hand and sped away out of the building. I stared after him open-mouthed. The gaoler was livid but there was nothing to be done without revealing the bribe. Foolishly I lingered to apologize but, furious at being duped, he gave me a push which sent me sprawling. As I tried to stand he cursed me soundly and kicked me so hard that I fell again. I curled into a ball and prayed he would not kill me. The appearance of another man saved me. I scrambled shakily to my feet and set off after Will.

He was waiting for me at the corner of the street.

"What happened to you?" he asked.

I told him and he looked suitably abashed. He returned the shilling saying he had no need of it. There were rich pickings wherever he looked.

"But you may be caught again," I protested.

"Not me!" he laughed. Then looking thoughtful said, "I may try my luck at the Cockpit. A small wager might bring its reward and I do like to see the feathers fly!"

I reminded him that the cockfighting, like most other sports, had been closed down by the authorities. He tapped the side of his nose. Did he know something I do not? There are ways and means, he told me, then darted away and was lost to view. Sadly, I must accept that he is a born thief. I uttered a short prayer that he may not come to an untimely end.

I pondered whether to redeem Papa's flagon but decided I might need the money. Somehow I had to find a horse and start the journey to Woolwich. I passed several livery stables but none could help me. Their horses were booked for days to come. I saw a carrier's sign but was told by a neighbour that the carrier was dead. The previous day he was set upon by two men who stole his horse and cart and left him lying senseless upon the cobbles.

I gave up and returned home where Poppet greeted me ecstatically. We spent a quiet evening. I vow to do better tomorrow.

August 18th

Today I am black and blue from the beating at the prison. I am stiff in my right leg but will survive. No time to feel sorry for myself.

91

The fires are now lit in the street and I must provide some kindling. I found some small logs in the yard and took them out to the nearest blaze. There is no breeze and the fires smoulder erratically. More smoke than flames. I came back into the house with my eyes smarting. Are the fires burning the pestilence from the air? Why do I doubt it?

I woke early with griping in my stomach and had no mind to seek out a horse today. I decided to rest and renew my flagging energies, which stood me in good stead for the doctor called on me. He had instructions on how to fumigate Aunt Nell's sick room, "Lest you return home at the end of the plague to find the disease still lingering."

He was pleased that I had obtained my certificate and urged me to be on my way out of London as soon as possible.

When he had gone I lit a small fire in the yard and burned the sheets from Aunt Nell's bed. On a whim I looked into her clothes chest and found her treasures, neatly wrapped in paper or cloth. A miniature of my grandmother, a spray of faded lavender, a bundle of letters which I did not read and a single letter that I did read. 'Twas from a man named Justin who wanted to marry Aunt Nell. Intrigued, I read on and then felt truly guilty. Poor Aunt Nell had apparently refused him, saying that she must care for me and Papa since my mother had died.

. . . I respect your wishes, dearest Eleanor, with a most heavy heart. Had you married me we could have raised the child as our own but since you confess that you care also for the widower I can do no more . . .

The discovery shocked me for I had known nothing of the romance with Justin. Nor had I the notion that Aunt Nell might have loved Papa. Has he ever known, I wonder? If so I assume he did not love her in return. After my mother's death he could have married Aunt Nell after a suitable interval. 'Tis strange to consider that I, too, might have had a different life. I might have been raised by Aunt Nell and Justin with the brothers and sisters that might have been born to them.

I sighed as I replaced the letter. Poor Aunt Nell might have led a very different life, too. I hope she didn't regret giving up Justin to care for us. How I *wish* I had been nicer to her.

I found also a small carved elephant which I shall keep for myself and take with me as a lucky charm. I know Aunt Nell would not object.

In the afternoon I went to the apothecary and bought amber, saltpetre and brimstone.

He said, "You are fumigating a room, I take it."

I told of Aunt Nell's death and he shook his head sorrowfully. "I am nearly out of such ingredients. Consider yourself fortunate." He then urged me to start the process as soon as possible.

"Keep the window shut tight for 24 hours then drive the smoke from the room with a flapping towel or small blanket."

I have done all that I was bid. I lit the fire in Aunt Nell's room and laid the brimstone, amber and saltpetre upon the glowing coals. It immediately sent out copious fumes which made me choke. I retired, closing the room behind me. I felt as though I was closing a door on my past life when I was happy and carefree. I wonder, will that time ever come again?

August 19th

I am writing this with my back propped against a tree about four miles from the city. My horse, Jasper, a grey cob, grazes nearby. He has a wild look in his eyes yet will not go above a snail's pace. I bought him for two shillings from the wife of a carter. Her husband has died of the plague and she wanted to be rid of the animal.

"The wretched creature bit me," she told me, "and would kick me if I went near enough. You are welcome to it. I've better things to do than go foraging for hay and oats!"

I had no money for the cart so I rode sidesaddle for nearly three hours with Aunt Nell's parasol to keep the sun from my head. My sweet little Poppet trotted alongside,

94

mighty puzzled at first by the horse and my sitting upon it. He whined for the first half hour but was finally resigned to the situation.

I may be tired and hungry (and I surely *am*) but I cannot claim to be lonely for the road is full of people making the same journey. We are all torn between hope and despair. All grateful to be among the living, but mostly mourning the dead.

One young man pushes his aged grandfather in a wheelbarrow for want of something better. Many make their escape on foot — a slow business. At least I am not reduced to that. A large wagon passed me bearing an enormous family. I counted twelve people crammed into it. Unless friends and neighbours are taking their chances together. Several young men of noble birth have also passed me, mounted upon fine horses, presumably their own. Other horses bear two riders, the second clutching the first around the waist. All have anxiety writ large in their eyes.

As I sit here writing, a few unfortunates are making their way in the other direction. These poor souls have been refused entry for one reason or another. They are full of dire warnings to the rest of us. They insist we will be turned back but I have my certificate safe in my pocket and have no fears on that score.

Poppet is happy now that I am descended to firm ground again and snuggles close to me. We have both eaten — a lump of bread and some cold mutton which I cooked yesterday. 'Twas hardly tender and I see that I must improve my cooking before anyone will want to wed me. If Aunt Nell told me that once, she told it a dozen times but I paid her no heed. Who now will help me be a good wife?

Next day

A few more miles between me and the poor stricken city. I wonder when I will see again the London I once knew, with cheerful crowds and the streets all a bustle. Around me now there is nought but grass and trees — and tents springing up like mushrooms. These belong to folk who have nowhere to go and no relatives to welcome them. They are camping out at what they hope is a safe distance from the contagion. Smoke rises from various fires and the air is full of cooking smells. A church nearby has struck seven but 'tis still as light as day and children run among the tents and play. I envy them. For the little ones 'tis no doubt a great adventure. For myself 'tis almost a torment.

I think the word for my condition is saddle-sore. How I wish I had taken my chances to ride more at Uncle John's. I am stiff in all my bones and joints and wish I need never set eyes on a horse again. Jasper truly is a bad-tempered animal, as the owner promised. He frequently stops for no reason and so abruptly that I am sometimes thrown from his back. When I try to climb up again he turns his head and tries to nip my leg. Twice he has stepped on my foot and once he has run away with me. He hates me. Of that I am certain.

Poppet is sad and sorry for himself. He picked a quarrel with a lurcher dog not an hour since and was soundly beaten. I had to leap from my horse to rescue him and almost lost my mount who chose to wander off while I was otherwise engaged. Poppet has a torn ear and has lost a tooth but I have no sympathy. He has only himself to blame. He seems to imagine the highway is his own and every other dog a trespasser.

I shall now wrap myself in my blanket and try to sleep a little. Jasper is tied to the lower branch of the tree against which I sleep. If it rains in the night I shall get wet for I have no cover except Aunt Nell's parasol which will serve me little in a downpour.

Later that night

I was woken to a great commotion. Upon enquiring, I was told that a man had fallen into a fit and died and an old woman was accused of bewitching him. Our family has always considered the idea of witchcraft as barbaric but I confess I was curious. I picked up Poppet and made my way into the circle and saw an elderly man lying on the grass. Beside him was an ugly old crone with a bent back. She was small and thin, her hair was straggly and her face was grey with fear. In truth she looked like a witch with few teeth and a shrill voice but I knew better. She was being roughly shaken by a large man of middle years. His clothes had seen better days and his chin was in dire need of a razor.

"You killed him," he insisted. "Confess, you evil old hag, or 'twill go hard with you."

The crowd cried out excitedly.

"Aye, confess."

"Bury her in the same grave. See how that becomes her."

"String her up. The wicked creature."

"She's the devil's handmaid, right enough."

The large man breathed hard and his eyes glittered with a kind of triumph.

"I'm no witch," the old woman cried fearfully. "I had naught to do with it."

I waited for someone to speak up for her but none did. As I looked at her birdlike frame, she reminded me fleetingly of poor Aunt Nell as she lay on her death bed. Scarcely knowing what I was doing, I pushed my way forward through the angry crowd.

"Let her be," I told them. "She is not to blame." I spoke up but my voice trembled. Of a sudden all eyes were on me.

The man glared at me. "What d'you know of the matter?"

" 'Tis common sense," I replied, for that was how Papa had argued it. He had also said witchcraft was for "gullible fools" but I dared not quote him exactly for fear of reprisals. I spoke as bravely as I could and looked straight at him without flinching but inside I was trembling.

"The man is dead of a fit," he insisted.

A woman spoke up. "She might turn her evil eye on the rest of us. On *you*, mayhap."

"She does not have an evil eye," I told her but even to my own ears my protestations sounded lamentably weak. Her innocence would be impossible to prove.

Ignoring me, the large man shook the old woman again and she began to sob, clasping her hands imploringly and begging for mercy in a thin whining voice. As I wondered what to do next another voice spoke up.

"The young woman speaks the truth. Belief in witchcraft is for the ignorant."

It was a young man, well bred. He wore a fine suit with a hat trimmed with a feather. The son of a wealthy merchant, perhaps. He looked at the large man whose face was turning an angry red. "You sir." He spoke mildly. "You look like an intelligent man. Release this old woman."

In truth the wretch looked just the opposite but I saw

99

at once how the young man hoped to solve the problem. Would the large man choose to brand himself ignorant? As he hesitated, the young man strode towards him, his hand outstretched. "Let us shake on it, as two intelligent men."

I doubt if the wretch had ever been called "intelligent" before and he liked the novelty. Before he knew what had happened they were shaking hands. At the same time there came a cry from someone in the crowd.

"Why look, the man is not dead. See, he has opened his eyes."

'Twas the truth. The man rubbed his eyes and then sat up. The assorted spectators muttered and crowded closer — except for the old woman. She took her chance and scuttled away and was quickly lost among the crowd.

They helped the man to his feet and marvelled at his recovery. Seeing that I could do no more I retired to write in my diary and shall now try to resume my sleep.

Probably August 21st

I was awoken by Poppet who was barking hysterically and opened my eyes to find the young man seated beside me, waiting for me to wake up. A large dark horse grazed nearby on a long rope which the man had wound around his arm. The man smiled and said his name was Marcus Wainwright. In the daylight I could see that his eyes were a very pale blue and his complexion smooth. His fair hair curled naturally beneath his hat. I sat up at once and rubbed at my face. I was mortified to be found so tousled yet pleased to see him. He said he admired my courage. Seeing that the man meant me no harm, Poppet made haste to greet him, wagging his tail in friendship. Master Wainwright stroked his ears and Poppet no longer had eyes for his poor mistress. So much for loyalty.

"I admired you also," I told Master Wainwright. "For the way you solved the problem. An intelligent fellow, you called him. That was cleverly done."

We both laughed. I was wishing I could brush my hair and clean my teeth. If only I had met him under more auspicious circumstances. Fate can be very unkind. "I am headed for Woolwich," I said, half hoping he went there too.

He, it seemed, had no fixed plan.

"I shall go where the mood takes me — as long as it is away from that accursed city."

I sprang to London's defence which made him laugh. Then he suggested we might travel on together. It was then that I made a frightful discovery. My horse was no longer tethered to the branch. I cried out in dismay, seeing at once how difficult my journey would be without him.

We made many enquiries but no one had seen the horse being led away. Rather, no one admitted it. I thought one or two looked shamefaced at my distress and think it likely they chose to look the other way. It seems where plague is a constant spectre, folk choose not to become involved. They try to remain isolated from their neighbours and who can blame them.

Without my horse I had lost my means of transport but at least I still possessed my Certificate of Health. My money was also safe for I kept it in my pocket beneath my skirts.

To my huge relief, Master Wainwright offered to share his horse and I happily accepted. (If I am honest, I was glad for the excuse to share a ride with so fine a young gentleman.) I wondered how old he was and whether he had a sweetheart — or worse, a wife. If not I wondered at his age. Would he wait for me to become a woman, I wondered. In six years I will be twenty and Papa would not hinder me. How jealous Maggie would be!

Master Wainwright's horse was a fine animal with a glossy chestnut coat and a flowing mane. His brown eyes were soft and intelligent. He was as different from my poor nag as chalk from cheese. With me riding behind, we set off on the last leg of our journey. Master Wainwright would deliver me to Woolwich, he told me, then continue alone to put a greater distance between himself and the city. He said that if I were willing, and in view of the exceptional circumstances, we might call each other by our given names. I agreed at once.

We stopped around midday and Master — that is Marcus

— gave me bread and cheese from the bag he carried across his back. We washed this down with a mouthful of ale and thought ourselves fortunate.

Meanwhile I was becoming alarmed by the number of people who were returning to London. I stopped one of the men who walked alone with his head down. He was the very picture of dejection, and I asked the reason for his retreat from Woolwich.

"Retreat, you call it? Aye, there's some truth in that." He eyed me gloomily. " 'Tis a dangerous situation. The wretches will not let us pass. With or without proof."

"Dangerous?" I stared at him, dismayed. "But we have certificates. What more do they need? I have an uncle — a farmer. He will give me shelter."

The man shook his head. "You'll find out for yourself in good time. They are quite beyond reason and look upon us all as a threat."

"But if I reason with them . . . If I explain . . ."

He gave a bitter laugh and walked on. I was shaken but unconvinced and Marcus and I set off again. It was late afternoon when we saw the first makeshift homes. Most were roughly fashioned from blankets and stakes. One or two at first but as the miles passed we saw many more. The truth dawned. The people who were refused entry to Woolwich must either camp out or return to London. I shuddered. This would be my fate if Uncle John would not vouch for me.

103

By early evening we were less than a mile from the town — I could see the houses and a church spire. I felt suddenly confident that all would be well. That I *would* convince them. That I *would* be allowed in. I imagined Uncle John greeting me with open arms.

Then we came to the barricade and my new-found confidence wavered. Felled trees had been dragged into place across the road and piled on either side. Behind this a group of angry looking men waited, some with drawn pistols, others with staves. Yet another brandished a sword. They were arguing with the people on our side of the barricade and their voices were loud with passion.

Marcus slipped from the horse's back and helped me down and we stood watching the ugly spectacle.

"You may show us a thousand certificates," one of the defenders shouted, "for they are not worth the paper they are written on. Half of them are forgeries. D'you take us for fools? Get back to London and take the plague with you."

I was suddenly furious and my rage gave me courage. With the help of my elbows, I worked myself to the front and produced my own certificate.

"This has been stamped and signed at the Old Bailey," I told them. "How dare you suggest 'tis a forgery."

"Oh lah," he replied, in mincing tones. "How dare you suggest 'tis a forgery. Just listen to her."

There was a murmur of solidarity from the far side of the

104

barrier but I refused to be beaten. I could not afford to be refused entry.

"Do you think," I answered, "that I would come so far without authentic documents? D'you take me for a fool?"

"Aye and worse than a fool," one of them replied, with a fearsome leer on his swarthy face. "You London folk make me sick. You are so superior when all goes well and think on us as country bumpkins. But come the sickness and you run to the country begging for our help."

His companions joined in a chorus of approval but I pressed on.

"Then send for my uncle, Farmer John Paynton. He shall vouch for me."

My voice shook with indignation, yet already there was a doubt growing within me. I could see determination writ large on their faces and in truth I hardly expected to win my point.

"Who are you to give us orders?" one of them shouted. "Hoity little maid, aren't you? We don't want the likes of you with your fancy clothes and big words. Full of airs and graces. We know your sort, so just take yourself off."

He thrust his fist hard into my chest and sent me flying backwards. Only the press of people behind me prevented me from falling.

"Get back where you belong," he roared and burst into loud laughter.

Another cried, "Aye. Get back to smoky London. Filthy

cobbles. Belching chimneys." To prove his disgust he spat in my direction but mercifully missed.

"He's right," came another voice. "Get yourself back to the smell of sickness and the cries of the dying. 'Tis all you're fit for."

I found my feet again, clutching at my chest where he had struck me. There were tears of pain and rage in my eyes which I tried to hide. I turned away and stumbled back to Marcus. He put a comforting arm around my shoulders. I told him of my defeat and he was shocked.

"Yet 'twas bravely done, little Alice," he told me but his kind words made the tears run faster. I sank to the grass verge and wept. Not solely for myself but for the tragedy being enacted around me. In truth I could see no end to the suffering. Aunt Nell had done well to die when she did, I thought despairingly, and nothing Marcus could say could comfort me.

August 22nd or 23rd

I know not which day 'tis and care less. I wish I had stayed at home for at least I had a roof over my head and a bed to sleep in. I asked God why he has done this to me and wonder if this is my punishment for killing Aunt Nell. But if so then what crimes have all the others committed?

106

I parted company with Marcus at first light as he had decided to move on, perhaps to Eltham. He begged me to accompany him but I have no business there and am determined to try again to reach Uncle John. Marcus left me a second small blanket which I take as a great kindness.

I wrote a note addressed to my uncle and sent it to him by hand. I had to trust somebody and chose a young lad with a mop of tow-coloured hair. He was loitering at the fringes of the crowd on the far side of the barricade. I gave him threepence by way of payment and can only pray he is honest. I begged Uncle John to come to the barricade to argue for my admittance. Pray God he comes. I take back all my criticisms of the farm and their way of life. All I want is to be off the road and safe within four walls. A good wash with soap — and one of Aunt Mary's stews would be bliss also. How precious the most simple pleasures seem once they are taken away from us.

I have had to tie Poppet up which he hates, poor sweet. He kept wandering off and once returned with a baby rabbit in his mouth. I had no fire, but a family nearby cooked it with a few carrots and offered me a share. I refused, saying that I should soon be fetched by my uncle. I thought they needed it more than I did. Later Poppet had another fight. This time 'twas a sheepdog and again he came off worst. His ear is torn and his front paw is bleeding. I am now afraid to allow him out of my sight.

The next day

Uncle John did not come. How could he desert me? I waited all day — until it was too late to make other plans. I was so sure he would speak up for me — the disappointment was terrible. But does he know I am here? Did the tow-headed boy deliver the note? Did Uncle John try to make contact or does he, too, fear that I am carrying the plague? Maybe they are resolved to take no risks. Aunt Mary may be afeared to take me in at such a late date. They have their own children to consider. 'Tis my own fault. I should have come earlier. How I regret not doing so. If we had left when Uncle John first wrote to us Aunt Nell would still be alive today and we would both be safe at the farm.

The next day

Early morning. I cried myself to sleep last night and now sit wretchedly alone. Confused and lonely and full of self-pity. I keep wondering how Marcus is faring. I hope he does better than I do.

Later the same day

Now I am totally bereft. Poppet chewed through the cord and ran away. I spent hours wandering in search of him but there is no sign. I thought nothing worse could happen but I was wrong. Most certainly he can feed himself — there are plenty of rabbits around, but will I ever see him again?

I am told 'tis August 25th

I am in a terrible fix. I have nothing and must make my way back to London to await Papa's release from the pesthouse. But what of Poppet? How can I abandon him? I spent most of the day searching for him without result. Some say they have seen him here or there but he has since disappeared completely. I have not eaten all day. To know that Uncle John is so near and cannot help me is a great frustration but I can see no help for it. I shall make one more attempt to convince the men at the barrier that my certificate is genuine. Then I shall give up.

Three hours later

No success at the barrier and Poppet is still missing. I hope God hears my prayers before I sleep. At daybreak I shall start the long walk back to London and pray I reach home safely.

August 27th

Yesterday, by the grace of God, my prayers were answered. Perhaps He is no longer displeased with me. After I had been walking homeward for most of the day I was hailed by a cheery cry. Turning, I saw Luke seated in his cart which already carried an elderly man, two haggard women and a child.

"By all that's wonderful," he cried. "'Tis young Alice Paynton."

He asked me if I wanted a ride home. I told him I had no money but would see him well paid by my father who

I hoped was recovering from the plague. This brought expressions of great alarm from those who rode with him. I showed them my certificate and they were at once reassured and helped me to climb up. Luke insisted that I share his seat and we talked at length, recounting our various adventures. We stopped once to rest the horse and allow it to crop the grass, then set off again at a good pace.

We came into the outskirts of London as the clocks struck one this morning. Sad to see the stricken city, yet I was pleased to be back. After Luke had deposited the others (they were one family) we rode on. The darkness was lessened by the light of the fires which still burn in the streets. We reached my home just before three this morning. Luke went on to his own house. I was left to fall into my bed, sadder and wiser than I had been on leaving it a week ago.

I slept until eleven and then ventured forth with one of Papa's leather-bound books on which I was lent a shilling. I managed to buy bread and milk and three eggs and made myself an omelette which I ate ravenously. How I wish I could have shared it with Poppet, but I still have no knowledge of his whereabouts. I watched for him constantly all the way home and made enquiries from all that we met but to no avail. The house is very quiet without him but I have sworn not to complain about anything. God has brought me back to my beloved city and I must be content.

August 29th

Bedtime and I am weary to my bones but the house is sparkling. Like a new pin, as Aunt Nell would have said. I have scrubbed and polished from top to bottom. Every cushion and blanket has been aired in the yard and every carpet has been thoroughly beaten. I am beginning to appreciate how hard Maggie worked. If she survives and returns to us, I shall persuade Papa to increase her wages.

August 31st

In truth I am the luckiest person in the world. I answered a knock at the door to find a stranger with a basket over his arm. He was a friend of Uncle John's, come into the city to attend briefly to some urgent business (he is a wool merchant). He would not venture inside the house tho' I assured him 'twas safe.

He handed over the basket and was at once gone on his

way. There was a jar of honey, some fresh churned butter and a goat's cheese. Also a leg of mutton and six beetroots. Tears of gratitude filled my eyes and I swear I shall never again say a harsh word against them nor shall any other. I daresay Uncle John has no knowledge of my attempt to enter Woolwich. Tomorrow I shall feast on meat and beetroot.

September 1st

Friday. Even knowing which day it is is a pleasure. When I look back on the confusions of my week away I can hardly believe I have survived. I think about Marcus Wainwright and wonder if he stayed in Eltham or moved southward into Kent. And the poor creature they called a witch — what of her? And my dear little dog. I make myself believe that some kindly soul has taken pity on him and cares for him. At least he is safe from the dog-catcher. I saw the wretch pass the house this morning and was tempted to empty the slops on to him.

113

September 2nd

I am counting the days until Papa is released. Then I shall wait outside for him lest he assumes me gone out of the city and makes for Woolwich.

September 4th

Papa is home again. I feel a peal of joyful bells should be rung. I waited outside the pesthouse and brought him home with me. He could scarcely walk he is so weak. 'Twill be long before he is restored to his former self. I did not know how to break the news of Aunt Nell's death but as soon as he asked after her I fell to weeping and he at once knew the truth. We comforted each other as best we could but 'tis sad to have no gravestone where we may lay flowers for her. No doubt when this is all over we could find where her body lies but 'tis a mass grave and I cannot face the thought of it.

September 6th

Wednesday, two o'clock — Papa has slept most of the morning. I made some soup with vegetables and barley which he found most welcome. He is still tormented by memories of the pesthouse of which he cannot or will not speak. The news of Aunt Nell's death has also mightily depressed his spirits and he speaks little except to answer my questions. I keep as cheerful as I can.

When I ventured out in search of milk and eggs I overheard two men discussing the Weekly Mortality Bills. It seems that this week nearly 7,000 people died of the plague which I find scarcely credible. Will there be anyone left? I did not tell Papa for fear of lowering his spirits further.

9 o'clock — Will called round to see if there was anybody in the house. I dared not ask him in but talked to him through the parlour window. Maggie has almost despaired of seeing me, believing that I was gone to Woolwich. I shall have so much to tell her. It seems they have received some poor relief but the money is spent and she is keen to have employment again. Her sister is recovered and being fourteen years old can manage alone. Will is as perky as ever he was. He offered to

cheer up my father with some jokes but Papa refused to see him. Will left promising to send Maggie to us tomorrow.

"And will you stay out of prison?" I begged him. "I cannot work a miracle every time they lock you up."

He grinned his perky smile. "I swear I'll do my best," he told me, hand on heart. "But I can promise nothing."

Sadly, he is a born rogue but a charming one.

Papa gave me some money and I retrieved the articles I had left with the moneylender. Papa will not accept that I am in any way to blame for Aunt Nell's death (which is a great comfort) and is full of praise for the way I cared for her.

September 11th

At last I have the strength to write in my diary again. I have been confined to bed since the day after Maggie returned. The doctor tells me 'tis the accumulated strain of the past few months which have overtaxed my body. The lack of food while I travelled to and from Woolwich made matters worse. Thank Heavens for Maggie who has been a tower of strength since I collapsed. I was chopping onions for a stew when I fainted clear away. I woke to find Maggie hauling me up the stairs to my bed.

By this time Papa had recovered a little and was up and about and sent Maggie straightway for the doctor. So now I am the invalid, but around me life is slowly returning to normal. Papa has ventured back to his office where work is haphazard as must be expected. Without Aunt Nell to talk to, Papa sits with me and tells me of his work which interests me greatly. Now that I am mistress in the house he treats me less like a child which is gratifying. In a strange way the plague has brought us closer together.

London is still in the grip of the plague, tho' the doctor insists it has reached its peak and must now slowly reduce in ferocity. He says that there are still many new cases but more folk are recovering from it. We must give thanks for small mercies.

September 17th

Lordsday — I am quite recovered and wish I could go to church. I want to kneel in our pew and give thanks in God's own house but Papa will not yet allow it. Instead I pray beside my bed and thank Him for my safety and for Papa's recovery. I do not speak to Him of my aunt for I do not wish to reproach Him. I still pine for my poor Poppet. I know

117

now that I will never see him again and Papa has promised me another dog once the plague is at an end. I said "Yes" to this but no other dog will ever take Poppet's place. He came to me as a present on the day I was nine and was my constant companion. Maggie says that when the plague ends there will be very few cats and dogs left alive which may make them costly.

I do not speak of my birthday which passed unnoticed. I doubt I shall ever have the pearls unless Papa remembers next year. Then I will be fifteen. Not old enough to be betrothed but wise enough to know when a suitable man comes along.

Papa sent Maggie up into the attic this morning where she found half a dozen pigeons roosting. Where they have come from I do not know but they seem quite at home. So tomorrow, if we can find a coal seller, we shall have a pigeon pie (I hope). I shall use Aunt Nell's book of recipes as Papa chooses not to trust Maggie's cooking. The days are still hot and I shall swelter with the heat from the fire but Papa feels we all need as much nourishment as possible. (Maggie says she feels like a goose being fattened for the Christmas table.) If only the weather would change. This has been such a hot and humid summer.

September 19th

God be praised. He has sent me back my little dog. I can scarce believe it but 'tis the truth. A knock came at the door around three o'clock this afternoon and I opened it to find Mistress Gratton on the doorstep. I stared at her as tho' at a ghost but then saw that she held Poppet under her arm. His lead was fastened securely round her hand.

"I believe this little rascal belongs to you," she said.

I was so taken aback I could not speak but took him into my arms and hugged him. There were tears in my eyes. He felt lighter and sadly neglected but was otherwise the same.

"I was returning from Dartford," Mistress Gratton continued, "and saw him running loose with two other dogs. I recognized him instantly. Do you remember when I was accosted by that lewd ruffian? Sweet Poppet laid his head in my lap and looked at me with such affection as tho' he tried to comfort me."

I nodded, too busy smothering Poppet with kisses to answer her with words.

"I knew at once how you would grieve for him," she went on, "so set about catching him."

She would not come into the house but we talked at

length. Her husband died of the plague in the pesthouse but, like me, she did not take it. So she had not been infected by the lewd wretch who kissed her. I stared at her and my heart leaped with relief. If she did not take the plague from that unwanted kiss, then the wretch was not infected. Therefore Aunt Nell could not have taken the contagion from contact with her or me. How she *did* take it is a mystery — unless 'twas during her journey to Southwark on the day her skirt was ruined. Poor Aunt Nell is still dead but *I* am not responsible for which I thank God most heartily.

I told Mistress Gratton of my attempt to reach Uncle John and the way in which I was forced home again. It seems she escaped London earlier — making her way to Dartford where her widowed sister — Mistress Bell — lives with her son, Edward, who is an apothecary. After much talk we parted company but are resolved to remain friends and to meet again when the city is itself again. How strange that she of all people should be the means by which I regained my sweet little dog. Had we not gone to her assistance, she would never have recognized Poppet and he would be lost to me forever.

September 21st

I forgot to say the pigeon pie was edible, tho' the crust was hard. (But I blame that on the times, for there was little butter for the pastry.) Still, it filled our stomachs for which God be praised. So many at this time are starving, homeless or sick. We must thank God we are preserved thus far.

September 24th

Little new to report but the joy of having Poppet with me. I wonder if he is as pleased as I am? I think of him romping in the fields with other stray dogs and catching a rabbit here and there. No doubt for him, after the confines of this house, it was a time of wonderful freedom. But he was in a sad state — his fur was tangled and so full of burrs that I was forced to cut some of them out. Then I bathed him and brushed him. He hated it but now looks himself again.

September 27th

Who should pass by but Master Winn, who was our watchman for a time. I was delighted to see him still hale and hearty. He has very little money and earns what he can running errands for the neighbours. He brought hopeful news that the worst of the plague is past. The doctors promise a decreasing death toll. Master Winn hopes that before another month is out his master may return and go about his business once more.

"I hope to be his manservant again," he told me. "When he abandoned me, I swore I would never return to him but he was a good enough master before he fled the city."

"There are so many dead," I said, seeking to cheer him. "Papa says there will be a great demand for servants and the like. You may be able to name your price."

"The same thought has occurred to me." He grinned and went on his way with my good wishes ringing in his ears.

November 21st

At last I have my diary to hand again. I have spent some weeks with Uncle John and the family and left this behind in its hiding place. As soon as the way was clear and the highways open Papa insisted that I should go to Woolwich to recuperate in the fresh air. I must confess I have enjoyed it better than I expected. Kate's baby — a little girl named Lizbeth — is a sweet child. She has blue eyes and very dark hair. I held her and she made no fuss. I think I shall like being a mother.

Sadly Jem, the baby's father, died of the plague (caught when their barge docked in the Thames). The child will be brought up by Aunt Mary as her own. Kate is full of melancholy but Aunt Mary says, " 'Tis only a broken heart and 'twill mend."

I found it strange to be among folk who have not lived through the plague and have no real understanding of it. They asked many questions about poor Aunt Nell's death which I did not care to dwell upon. Poppet was happy to be back in the country but I did not once take my eyes from him lest he disappear again. In the main 'twas a restful time but I am mighty pleased to be back in London where I belong.

The doctors' hopeful forecast was proved correct. The weekly death toll plummeted rapidly towards the end of October and has been falling ever since. 'Twill not be finally over until the cold weather puts an end to the contagion but already people are coming back to London.

December 1st

I have less and less time to write in my diary now that I must take Aunt Nell's place in the household. Cooking, shopping, cleaning . . . Even with Maggie's help 'tis amazing how the hours fly by. I fall into bed each night and sleep at once.

Only a few weeks and Christmas will be with us again. Life is slowly returning to normal. A few of the street-sellers are once again calling their wares in the street. Rain has finally washed the dirt away so that the city looks clean again. There are many, however, without employment and some of these are set to work to pull weeds from the cobbled streets. Others beg.

Mistress Capperly returned two days ago from Dorking and brought a black kitten with her in a basket. (Her ginger cat disappeared during the summer and is most likely caught by the dog-catcher tho' we did not speak of this to her.) The kitten's name is Sooty which made Papa laugh for the first time in months.

"How very original," he said and laughed until the tears ran. He wiped his eyes but fell to laughing again and could not stop. Maggie and I exchanged looks for 'twas hardly *that* funny but we were pleased to see him happier than of late. He still grieves for Aunt Nell as I do. I am now moved into her bedchamber which is larger than my attic room (which meant finding a new hiding place for this diary). I have no likeness of her but I have hung her favourite bonnet on a hook above my mantelpiece and keep a small posy of rosemary below it by way of remembrance.

Luke called in to see me which made Maggie jealous tho' why I know not since her Jon has survived. Luke is rehearsing his lines for a play to be produced at the Dukes Theatre in January. (Meanwhile he has bought a cart with the money he made during the plague and is available for hire as a carter while he waits to become famous on stage.) In fact he has only ten lines in the play but is very proud of the part. He recited all ten lines to us with suitable actions. Papa has promised that we can go to see him when the play opens in the New Year.

I wonder what 1666 will bring to us?

August 5th, 1666

Lordsday. To St Andrew's. A long, long sermon. I have sadly neglected my diary in the excitement of meeting Edward Bell which I did some months ago. The day was January 9th and is imprinted on my heart forever. Quite by chance, I was walking with Maggie to the river to meet her Jon. We were meant to go straightway to the market but Maggie cannot bear to let a day pass without seeing him. At first I thought this romantic and then foolish but now I understand. I wish that Edward lived in London instead of Dartford.

(His latest letter ends with four kisses. It starts "My most sweet Alice" and ends "From your devoted Edward." I cannot ask for more.)

As Maggie and Jon exchanged sly kisses and I waited idly beside the boat steps, who should I see but Mistress Gratton. She was alighting from a wherry and with her was a young man. Not tall but not short, yet sturdily built with fine dark curls and brown eyes. Edward, her nephew, is 21 years old and loves me to distraction as I do him. But on that first day I did not pay him much heed for he is not exactly handsome though he has a fine mouth and good teeth. Aunt Nell was

126

wont to say "Handsome is as handsome does." I never did know what she meant but to me 'tis the man I love and not his face. (In truth I am not exactly perfect myself.) But Edward has a sweet nature and makes me laugh.

We exchange letters and meet occasionally. Papa and I have supped with Mistress Gratton, Mistress Bell (Edward's mother) and Edward and they have visited with us. Edward's widowed mother has taken over her husband's apothecary while Edward still studies. She impresses me greatly for she can add a column of figures as fast as any man. Nothing deters her. She buys in the medicaments from far and wide and deals with doctors and patients alike in a most businesslike way. For the present she employs an elderly assistant but one day Edward will work with her. He can already read and write in Latin and is studying herbs and other medicaments. I, too, have decided to learn what I can. (I learned the Latin verb "to love." *Amo, amas, amat* . . . I tell him I do not need more.) I am also reading from some of Edward's books and find them fascinating. If plague ever comes again I shall find it strange to stand on the other side of the apothecary's counter.

Papa approves of Edward and knows how much I hope to marry him when I am old enough. He is eager for the match and anxious too that I should be worthy. For my birthday he gave me a year's dancing lessons. I never did receive my promised pearls because the plague intervened to cause

127

havoc with Papa's employment. (For the weeks he was ill he received no payment.) But I am older and wiser and know that to be without pearls is scarcely a hardship when others in the world have so little.

Papa is once more engrossed in his work and late home from his office most days. We still have Maggie tho' she will leave us as soon as she is with child. I do most of the cooking which I now practise most diligently for the day when (I hope) I shall be Mistress Bell. With such a scholarly husband we shall doubtless entertain and I must have some recipes which cannot go awry in the cooking.

On Saturday Papa and I go by hackney to Dartford. 'Tis Mistress Bell's birthday and we shall walk in the fields if the weather is fine and eat a supper with them. Last time we did so, we made music with them after (Edward has a fine voice) and returned late which pleased me. 'Tis always an adventure to travel at night.

September 2nd

Lordsday. We returned from a short visit to Uncle John's very early this morning. Although the moon was out we were amazed to see a bright glow in the sky above the river. As we drew near the river the driver of the carriage cried out, pointing across the water.

"See there. Close to the bridge. Another fire."

We saw at once that he was right. Fires are not uncommon where wooden houses are crammed close. By the direction of it, Papa thought it in New Fish Street or Pudding Lane above Thames Street. We took to the river and made our usual crossing, admiring the dazzle of flames reflected in the water. Papa shook his head, saying that the buildings would burn like a funeral pyre by reason of the pitch that covers all the wooden beams.

We came home. I am too tired to write more.

Later the same day

Up again to church to find much excitement among the congregation. It seems the fire we saw earlier still burns and has spread. The rumour was whispered from pew to pew that the blaze was started by a Papist hoping to destroy the city. Another rumour we heard on the way into the church claims 'twas an accident started in a baker's oven. They say the fire was not properly drawn after baking bread and re-ignited while the baker slept. It seems that the poor man, (Farynor by name), escaped with his family by way of the roof but a maidservant died. Papa believes this to be the true version. (But if 'tis the Papist then I hope they can arrest the wretch.)

On leaving the church we made our way towards the blaze but could not get near enough except to see smoke billowing up from the area. The thoroughfares were clogged with people carrying their goods and chattels away from the fire. They say 'tis spreading and has consumed an inn and St Margaret's church in Fish Street. The wind is strong from the east and everywhere about us in the air there were sparks and large burning flakes which might be paper or cloth.

When we reached home we could still smell smoke.

We were eating our midday meal when Mistress Capperly came in greatly distressed. She told us the fire was quite out of control and had spread on to London Bridge. We looked at her with horror.

"The houses on the bridge are all ablaze," she told us, "and falling into the water. The streets are thronged with people, carts and carriages, all laden with furniture, bedding and clothes. Everywhere people are fleeing their homes."

She held a hand to her heart and breathed deeply.

I said, "Luke will be busy. He now has his own horse and cart."

"Then he will make another fortune," she cried, "People are paying five and ten pounds to have valuable goods carried to safety."

This was such a large sum I thought she exaggerated but said nothing.

Papa's colleague, Master Waybold, lives off Philpot Lane, nearby the area of the fire, and Papa decided he must make his way there and offer help. He told Maggie and I that we were to stay in the house and departed with much haste.

Mistress Capperly returned to her own house and Maggie and I cleared the table and washed the dishes.

Maggie grinned. "How will he know where we are? As long as we are home before he returns."

Thinking myself no more a child, I nodded. Aunt Nell would have needed no permission. "I was thinking the selfsame thing," I told Maggie.

We slipped from the house and were at once aware of the heavy pall of smoke that hung above the city, hiding the sun. A fine grey ash fell like a soft rain and we shielded our faces with our hands for fear of breathing it in. As we hurried towards the water in search of Jon we could hear the dull roar of the flames. I felt a prickle of unease but said nothing. Together we pushed our way to the front of the crowd that thronged the boat stairs but there was no sign of Jon. Instead we saw a scene which rivalled the worst days of the plague. The riverside was littered with bags, boxes and items of furniture. More was being unloaded from carts and wagons. Faces were grimy with smoke and dust and many were streaked with tears. All eyes were wide with fear

131

as the boats jostled for position. They left the stairs, heavily loaded with goods as others arrived empty to be immediately fought over by the desperate crowd.

"There he is," cried Maggie and we saw Jon passing, his boat as loaded as the next. Maggie waved but he did not see her. "He, too, will make his fortune by this evening."

Beside me an elderly man clutched a rolled bundle of blankets and pillow. A sudden surge in the crowd knocked him sideways and, losing his balance, he fell into the water with a cry of terror.

"Save me!" he screamed.

His wig floated free and some heartless wretches laughed at the sight. I crouched down, reaching out my hand for his but the distance was too great. He would not release his hold on the bedding and was rapidly carried some yards from the landing stairs.

"Help him," I shouted, turning to face the men in the crowd. "Pull him from the water."

His expression was one of extreme terror but the bundle was keeping him afloat.

"He'll be run down by a boat," cried Maggie. "Or crushed between two of them."

It seemed very likely. I wished I could swim but knew that to go in after him would mean certain death for both of us. Fortunately, at that moment, a young man pushed his way forward and dived into the swiftly flowing water. A great cheer

132

went up from the crowd as the rescuer reached the drowning man and brought him to safety further along the bank.

I straightway moved back from the water's edge lest I be the next one to fall in. I was very shaken by the incident for it brought back some of the horrors of last year's plague when death was an everyday occurrence. I knew that we should have stayed at home and blamed myself for allowing a maidservant to take such foolish risks.

"We cannot stay here," I told her and pushed my way back up the steps dragging Maggie by the hand.

We went elsewhere but could only draw near to the fire by fighting against the press of people who stumbled about in panic. We saw the Lord Mayor and several Aldermen but they, too, seemed unsure what to do.

"Pull down some houses," a man urged them. "Create a barrier for the fire. Then the flames will not jump from one house to the next. Pull them down, I say. Order it now."

But the mayor hesitated saying that if he did so the town would be liable for the cost of rebuilding them and that would be a heavy burden. We loitered, waiting on his decision and after much argument it was agreed. Three houses were chosen for demolition and willing men were organized. With long metal firehooks they gripped projections in the structure of the first house and began to shout.

"Stand clear."

"Back. Further back."

We needed no second bidding and moved well back. They tugged and tugged as sweat ran down their faces. Suddenly a gable loosened and swayed forward. Then the top half of the façade, the front of the building, fell into the street with a crash. It sent up clouds of dust which set us coughing. Fragments of plaster flew and bounced in all directions. One of the men was struck on the arm by a piece of debris and cursed as blood began to flow from the wound.

"We've seen enough, Maggie," I said firmly. Ignoring her pleas, I moved away. Maggie followed reluctantly, glancing over her shoulder all the while.

"They were too late," she cried. "See how the flames have jumped the gap."

I nodded but I longed to be gone from the scene. The heat was intense, my throat was painfully dry and my eyes hurt. We made our way thankfully home.

Papa returned, exhausted. The Waybolds have fled the city with their valuables, for unless the wind changes direction their home may soon be consumed by the flames. They pray their house will still stand on their return but Papa fears the worst. The Mayor is to call out the Trained Bands to keep order and prevent looting.

Late that same day

I took Poppet for a walk to hear news of the fire and came almost at once on a small crowd. They were listening to a large, swarthy woman who was haranguing them. She carried a bundle of goods on her head and carried pots and pans tied across her shoulders.

"Believe me or believe me not but I speak the truth. The Dutch have fired London by way of revenge and have burnt our houses to the ground. Mine's gone and—"

"Revenge for what?" asked a young woman who carried a baby in her arms.

The speaker rolled her eyes, despairing of the woman's ignorance. "Why, for our successes at sea. Can't you understand? Didn't our sailors win a mighty victory over their fleet? Hundreds of our sailors set fire to their ships in Brandaris and burned the town. We killed thousands of their men."

I said nothing but I had heard this rumour from Papa who heard it from Master Pepys.

A young man asked why he had heard nothing of the affair.

" 'Cos you don't listen," she cried, wagging a finger at him. "My son's a sailor under Prince Rupert and he told me."

135

She looked around in triumph. "Now they send mischief makers to fire London. And such as me are on their way to Moorfields because I've no roof over my head. Thank the Lord for fine weather for we'll sleep under the stars tonight."

She turned on her heel and strode away and for a moment the crowd watched her go in silence. Moorfields. I thought about the laundry that is daily spread to dry there. 'Tis hoped the owners collected it long since for the falling ash would dirty it again. We are fortunate to have a small yard in which to dry our washing.

One said, "We should pray for rain to douse the flames."

We eyed each other nervously.

An elderly man shook his head. "*I* heard tell 'twas the Papists."

I asked him, "But what grudge do *they* have against us? They live among us in friendship."

Now everyone hung on his words as he tapped the side of his nose with a stubby finger. "Friendship?" He sucked in breath. "Never trust a Papist. They want a Catholic country. *That's* their grudge. If that's what you want to call it. Me, I call it a plot. They want England the way 'twas before King Henry the Eighth broke with the Pope. They've been waiting for their chance and now they've got it."

All around me angry murmurs broke out.

"But the fire was started accidentally," I protested hastily

136

for the talk was beginning to alarm me. "In a baker's shop in Pudding Lane."

He tossed his head. "So it did, but who started the baker's fire? He swears he had raked out his oven before he went to his bed. I've heard they've arrested several Papists who were seen to throw burning fireballs in to the churches. They thought to get away scot free but were seen and accused."

Poppet chose that moment to chase after a cat, nearly jerking my arm from its socket, so that I heard no more of the accusations. I shall ask Papa what more he knows when he returns from his office.

To my surprise I learned that the fire, far from being out, was *still* burning and growing stronger. No longer confined to the riverside but being blown north by a changed wind. Folk said it was all along Thames Street and westward. If it should go east and reach Cheapside it seems the goldsmiths will be hard put to save their valuables. I walked nearer but found it uncomfortable going. The air was hot to breathe and full of ash and burning flakes which swirled in the air. The smell of burning wood was unmistakable and there is a dull roar in the background as the flames and heat rise skyward. The huge pall of smoke drifts overhead, so that even the sun's light is dimmed. Panic is in the air and on every face there is a mixture of despair and loss. The latter not only for

137

personal possessions but for London, which some swear is one third burned away.

I returned home to eat a thin and tasteless stew which Maggie had prepared. She was in a bad humour, complaining that, being confined to the house, she is missing all the excitement. I write this sitting on my bed with Poppet beside me. I hope there are no dogs and cats burned by the fire. There most certainly will be many homeless animals after this.

Ten o'clock the same day

My head aches abominably and my shoulder is badly bruised but I will come to that . . .

After the meal I gave in to my curiosity and Maggie and I ventured out. Maggie had cheese and bread in a cloth and was determined to find Jon Ruddle, insisting he will have no time to find food. I was hoping for a letter from my own dear Edward but 'tis now unlikely. Overnight the Post Office at Dowgate was taken by the fire. I wonder what Edward thinks of the fire. No doubt he will worry about me and pray for my safety as I do for his.

I hoped we might get closer to the fire but the press of people in the streets made it impossible — men and women

138

scurrying hither and thither with what belongings they could salvage. The narrow streets were crammed to bursting and most people are frightened, angry or confused. The Mayor has now called in the Trained Bands to help wherever they can. We learned also that King Charles himself is in the midst of it. His beautiful clothes are blackened with soot and his fine boots ruined from the water with which they try to douse the flames. Elsewhere they said that the Duke of York is helping also, passing buckets of water as part of a chain.

I parted company with Maggie, who made her way to the river, while I, having had enough of disaster for one day, headed towards home. Why, I wondered, was God punishing us yet again? Whatever our sins, we should all pray for forgiveness. I thought to spend a few moments in earnest prayer and without more ado entered the first church I came to. To my surprise 'twas quite noisy, being filled with refugees from the fire. They sat in dazed groups but some were alone, surrounded by their belongings, and many were red-eyed from weeping. I felt like an intruder and would have fled but at that moment a scuffle broke out near the font close to where I stood.

All heads turned but, sunk in lethargy and hopelessness, no one moved. I saw a poor woman clinging to a large bundle which a burly ruffian was trying to take from her. He was dishevelled with a bushy beard and very little hair. I clutched his sleeve. He jerked his elbow into my stomach

139

which winded me for a moment but I returned to the fray, more angry now than frightened.

"Leave her be," I shouted, "or I shall call for your arrest."

For my impudence he slapped me across the mouth and I felt the sour taste of blood which startled me. (My lip was cut by a tooth.) The woman began to scream at him but with a final tug he wrested the bundle from her and turned to run away. I again caught hold of his arm and held on grimly so that my weight hindered him. He turned with an oath and punched me on the side of my face. As I stumbled, he kicked my shin for good measure.

By this time another man was making his way up the aisle in our direction. Seeing that help was on its way I grabbed the bundle and clung to it like a leech. The wretch thrust out an arm and threw me backwards so that I fell against the stone font. I struck my head and lost consciousness. When I regained my wits, the wretch had been caught and held and was dragged away to be delivered to the authorities. The woman was once more clutching her belongings. She smiled down at me as she wiped away her tears and mumbled her thanks. The bundle contained all that she owned in the world now that the fire had burned her home by the river. Our rescuer helped me to my feet.

"This is all I have in the world," she told me as her eyes filled once more with tears. "I watched my home burn. 'Tis no more than charred wooden beams upon the ground."

Here she gulped for air. "All that remains is the brick chimney stack."

I could imagine the sight, a forest of sooty chimneys where once there were dwellings. My own tears were not far away as we made our farewells. Still a little dazed, I made my way home.

So now I ache in various places, my jaw is swollen and my lip is split but will heal. Papa was horrified when he saw me but not surprised by my story. It seems thieves are flocking to the city to take advantage of the chaos and steal where they may. Please God the fire will be out by morning. I am thankful that Edward will not see me in this sorry state.

Mistress Capperly knocked on our door, searching for Sooty, and discovered him in our yard. Hearing of my struggle in the church she took me to her house and gave me a dish of lemon cream which slipped down easily and eased my parched throat.

Papa returned late saying that Lord Craven has been charged by the King to organize further demolition of houses. They hope to starve the fire and will do all else necessary for the protection of the people.

"He will do all that is needful," he told us. "I have the highest opinion of the man. He stood by us throughout the plague when others had fled. Londoners owe the man a great debt of gratitude."

Papa believes the worst is over. By morning the fire should be under control.

September 4th

Tuesday. London still burns. I can scarce believe it. Today Papa was not required at the office so he and I ventured out together. We spent more than an hour watching the tragic end of London's greatest church which was a great sorrow to us. St Paul's has burned all day, fanned by a rising wind. We were told it first caught at the top, and the wooden roof timbers were soon ablaze. We spoke with one of the stonemasons who had worked on it from time to time, doing small repairs.

"I would have wagered any money St Paul's would survive," he told us, shaking his head as we all watched from a safe distance. "But no. See how the stones grow hot and split asunder. And see, too, the lead melts and drips down inside the church."

Even as he spoke the roof caved in with a fearful crash. It made the ground shake under our feet and filled the air with burning dust that threatened to choke us. We backed away sick at heart, yet none could turn their back on the dreadful spectacle. London's St Paul's was being destroyed before our eyes. Surely this was a sign from God. I hoped it *wasn't* the work of our enemies. If 'twas they would be celebrating in earnest. As the stonework fell it exploded on landing, sending hot splinters of stone in all directions. Merely watching the destruction was becoming dangerous. Papa decided I had suffered enough the day before and insisted that we leave the scene.

We made our way down to the riverside where all that remained of the pitiful houses were the chimneys that still stood among the black and smouldering embers. I thought of the woman in the church and wondered what had become of her.

"A good riddance to the houses," Papa remarked. "They were rat-infested hovels."

"But where will the people live?"

"The authorities will have to rebuild and they will build better. Homes fit to live in."

He seemed mighty sure so I did not argue but hoped he was right. Chastened, we returned home to a supper of cold rabbit pie, which was all Maggie could offer with the markets in a turmoil and few street sellers. I went to bed too tired to dwell on the problem. Will the fire ever stop?

Wednesday

A great excitement for me. Shortly before midday I was in the yard brushing Poppet when who should appear beside me

143

but my own dear Edward. I leaped to my feet and threw my arms around his neck. He was so pleased to see me safe and well — except for my bruises and split lip. He had brought some eggs and vegetables which were most welcome — and some medicaments. He says their apothecary has all but sold out of salves for burns and soothing jellies for parched throats. So many apothecaries have been destroyed that folk are going further afield in search of medicaments.

My letter from him went astray — probably consumed by the flames as I suspected. But to see my betrothed in person was a greater joy. I took him into the parlour away from Maggie's flapping ears and regaled him with tales of the past few days.

"But the fire is on the wane at last," he told me. " 'Tis under control. It still blazes in parts but is greatly reduced. The wind has dropped and they are busy damping down the embers. Everywhere is burnt timber and blackened stones but we have seen the worst of it. From now on we must look forward and not backward. There will be no time for regrets."

He sounded like Papa. He asked if I wanted to venture out with him but I said I had seen enough. To sit at ease with him in the comfort of the parlour was all I wanted. So we sat for an hour or more until he had to leave. He was on his way to see his aunt, Mistress Gratton, and to stay overnight. On the way out he whispered that he loved me and that he had a question to put to Papa later in the day.

144

He would say no more so that I was in a tizzy for hours and Maggie threatened to "shake a little sense into me." But, true to his word, he returned around eight and asked Papa formally for my hand in marriage — *when* I was old enough. Papa hesitated but finally he said "Yes" — as long as I am still of the same mind in three years' time. There will be no need to find accommodation, for his family has rooms above the apothecary and I am more than willing to share them with Edward's mother and to learn from her.

Now I am the happiest girl in the world. We invited Mistress Capperly to join us in a glass of wine by way of celebration. Next week we shall invite Mistress Gratton, Edward and his mother for supper and share a little music. How I wish Aunt Nell could be with us.

She would be so happy for me. I said as much to Papa. "If Aunt Nell could be with us life would be perfect." He smiled. "A perfect life would be of little value." I should have expected that. He believes that we learn by our mistakes and grow strong by suffering. I know he is right but at least some of the bad times are over. The city has suffered mightily these past few years but I have survived with God's help. London will rise again from the ashes and I look forward to the future with hope in my heart — and with my dearest Edward by my side.

Historical note

London was an important and prosperous city in the seventeenth century. However, despite the impressive buildings and many beautiful churches, most of the population lived in narrow streets in timber-framed houses. These dwellings were crowded together and conditions were, by modern standards, very uncomfortable. There was little drainage or sanitation and rubbish was collected from the cobbled streets by "scavengers" who raked it up daily and removed it to large pits in the city's outskirts.

Unfortunately, most of the time the rubbish, including scraps of food, was left lying about, and this encouraged rats. They were a common sight and no one gave them a second glance, but these rats carried fleas, which in turn carried the deadly bubonic plague. People spent a lot of time and energy trying to get fleas out of their furnishings, clothes and hair without success. When rats from a country with plague entered England on ships, their fleas soon began to infect people and bubonic plague broke out.

This is what happened in London in 1665. The populace,

147

ignorant of the causes of the disease, went about their daily lives, unaware that disaster loomed.

After the Great Fire of London in 1666 hundreds of new houses were built and new buildings were made of brick. These were not so easily inhabited by rats, which meant that, over time, widespread plague would become a thing of the past.

Alice's diary is fictional, but both men and women kept diaries in the seventeenth century and many have survived. Samuel Pepys and John Evelyn both wrote about living in London during the seventeenth century and the former has become a classic.

For women who could read and write, "books of household remedies" were kept and added to regularly. Most small wounds and minor illnesses were dealt with at home where women used herbs to treat many common ailments. Hospitals were few, and operations were performed without anaesthetics as we know them today. Great faith was placed in astrology, and superstition was widespread. Fake or unqualified doctors flourished, especially during the plagues.

There were many forms of entertainment. You could visit theatres on both sides of the river, including The Globe where many of Shakespeare's plays were performed. People played instruments — the virginals, viols and lutes were popular — and composed songs. Those who could afford it took singing and dancing lessons. Poorer people went to fairs, both large and small, or watched jugglers, stilt walkers and acrobats performing in the streets. Wrestling also had a large following. Many "entertainments" involved animals: a dancing bear was a common sight, bulls were baited by dogs for people's amusement, cockfighting was popular for men who liked to gamble, and so was horse racing.

Food was plentiful and varied for most people. When housekeeping was sufficient, large amounts of meat, fowl and game were eaten, washed down by French wines. The poor ate bread, mutton, bacon or cheese with their home brewed ale. No one drank water if they could avoid it because it was full of impurities. Recipes survive of fruit puddings and tarts, jellies and "creams." Fish was plentiful and oysters were cheap. Many people earned their living as "street criers." They carried foodstuffs such as pies or oranges in trays on their heads or in baskets over their arms. They "sang" their wares aloud to alert the housewives and servants that they were coming.

London provided a livelihood, too, for the countless farmers who lived in the surrounding areas. Most of them brought produce in daily to sell in the markets so that fresh eggs, cream, chickens, honey and vegetables could be brought fresh to the table. The docks were another source of thriving commerce with ships sailing in and out from other parts of England as well as from abroad. Timber, coal, cotton, spices and many other necessities were brought to London in sailing ships of every kind. Along the congested riverbanks, warehouses abounded where many highly inflammable goods were stored. The River Thames was also the quickest way to move from one part of London to the other and boats known as wherries were always for hire, waiting at the numerous "boat stairs" to take passengers up, down or across the river.

The seventeenth century was a troubled period politically. Britain was ruled by Parliament as well as a monarchy and there were constant disagreements over the way the country should be governed and taxed. Matters between Parliament and the monarchy grew steadily worse. Eventually few Londoners supported King Charles I and he went to York where he had powerful friends. The Civil War broke out and when it ended King Charles was arrested and executed and Oliver Cromwell declared himself Lord Protector in place of a king.

When Cromwell died, Charles II was invited to return as King, although the real power remained with Parliament. Charles II was still on the throne when the Great Plague ravaged London in 1665 and when, a year later, the Great Fire destroyed most of the city.

The country was officially Protestant and people of other faiths were regarded with the same suspicion as foreigners.

During the period of the Great Plague and Fire, England was at war with either France or Holland or both. Foreigners and Catholics were often blamed for disasters like these.

Alice's London was a rough, noisy, bustling place where more than eighty churches rang their bells. During the Great Plague more than 60,000 people died (around a third to a half of the population of London at that time) and the survivors had to rebuild their shattered lives. After the Great Fire more than 100,000 people were left homeless (though luckily there were very few deaths). Half the city was burned to the ground and it, too, would have to be rebuilt. It would be a more modern city and it would thrive again — but Alice Paynton's London had gone forever.

Timeline

1603 Queen Elizabeth I dies. James VI of Scotland becomes King James I of England.

1605 Gunpowder Plot. Guy Fawkes tries to blow up Parliament and James I. He fails and is executed.

1611 The King James version of the Bible is finished.

1620 Pilgrims land at Plymouth Rock, America, in their ship the *Mayflower*.

1625 Charles I becomes king.

1633 Samuel Pepys (1633–1703), the famous diarist is born.

1645 The Civil War. Oliver Cromwell forms the New Model Army. Charles I is defeated.

1649 Charles I is tried and executed. The Commonwealth is set up and lasts until 1660.

1653 Cromwell becomes Lord Protector.

1658 Cromwell dies.

1660 Charles II is restored to the throne.

1665 The Great Plague.

1666 September 2nd–5th. The Great Fire of London.

1667 The Dutch fleet defeats the English in the River Medway.

1685 James II becomes King of England.

1688 The "Glorious Revolution." James II is overthrown and he escapes to France.

1689 William III and Mary II become King and Queen of England.

Picture acknowledgments

The Diseases and Casualties this Week.

		Imposthume	11
		Infants	16
		Killed by a fall from the Belfrey at Alhallows the Great	1
		Kingsevil	2
		Lethargy	1
		Palsie	1
		Plague	7165
Abortive	5	Rickets	17
Aged	43	Rising of the Lights	11
Ague	2	Scowring	5
Apoplexie	1	Scurvy	2
Bleeding	2	Spleen	1
Burnt in his Bed by a Candle at St. Giles Cripplegate	1	Spotted Feaver	101
		Stilborn	17
Canker	1	Stone	2
Childbed	42	Stopping of the stomach	9
Chrisomes	18	Strangury	1
Consumption	134	Suddenly	1
Convulsion	64	Surfeit	49
Cough	2	Teeth	121
Dropsie	33	Thrush	5
Feaver	309	Timpany	1
Flox and Small-pox	5	Tissick	11
Frighted	3	Vomiting	3
Gowt	1	Winde	3
Grief	3	Wormes	15
Griping in the Guts	51		
Jaundies	5		

Christned { Males — 95 | Females — 81 | In all — 176 }
Buried { Males — 4095 | Females — 4202 | In all — 8297 } Plague — 7165

Increased in the Burials this Week ———— 607
Parishes clear of the Plague ——— 4 Parishes Infected ——— 126

The Assize of Bread set forth by Order of the Lord Maior and Court of Aldermen, A penny Wheaten Loaf to contain Nine Ounces and a half, and three half-penny White Loaves the like weight.

Bills of Mortality were published every week in London in 1665. The bills show how many people had died and what diseases they died of. This bill shows that 7,165 people died from the plague in one week alone.

154

The top scene shows plague victims in a house (a coffin lies ready on the floor). The middle picture shows a procession of people leaving the city to escape the plague. In the third scene, people are being buried in mass graves.

155

A doctor in his protective suit. The long beak section would have contained herbs that were believed to be protection against the plague.

This woodcut shows a "dead cart" arriving at a graveyard. The driver rang a bell to warn people he was coming and shouted, "Bring out your dead."

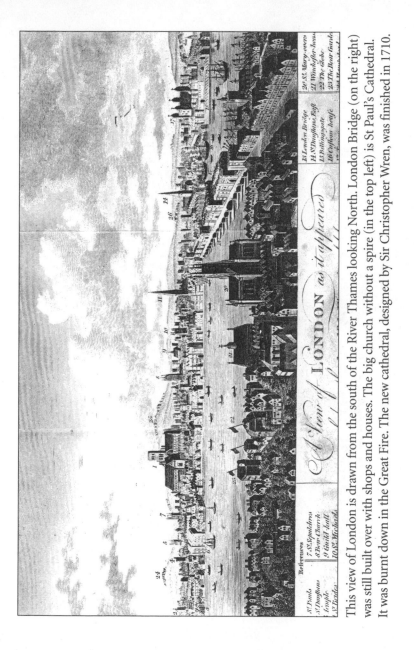

This view of London is drawn from the south of the River Thames looking North. London Bridge (on the right) was still built over with shops and houses. The big church without a spire (in the top left) is St Paul's Cathedral. It was burnt down in the Great Fire. The new cathedral, designed by Sir Christopher Wren, was finished in 1710.

157

Experience history first-hand with My Story –
a series of vividly imagined accounts of life in the past.

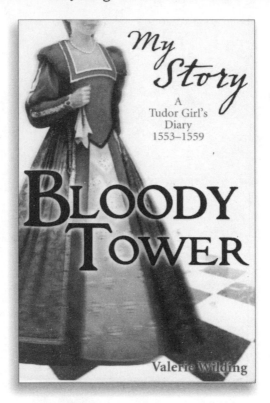

My Story
A Tudor Girl's Diary 1553–1559
BLOODY TOWER
Valerie Wilding

Tilly lives in turbulent times. It's the 1550s and,
when Queen Mary ousts Lady Jane Grey to
win the throne, her executioners are kept busy. Even
Princess Elizabeth is imprisoned in the Tower.
As Tilly watches the plots and politics of the
Tudor court unfolding, she waits for her chance
to deliver a very important letter . . .